A Load of Old Tripe

Also by Gervase Phinn

THE DALES SERIES

The Other Side of the Dale
Over Hill and Dale
Head Over Heels in the Dales
Up and Down in the Dales
The Heart of the Dales

A Wayne in a Manger
Twinkle, Twinkle, Little Stars

POETRY

published by Puffin Books

It Takes One to Know One
The Day Our Teacher Went Batty
Family Phantoms
Don't Tell the Teacher

A Load of Old Tripe

GERVASE PHINN

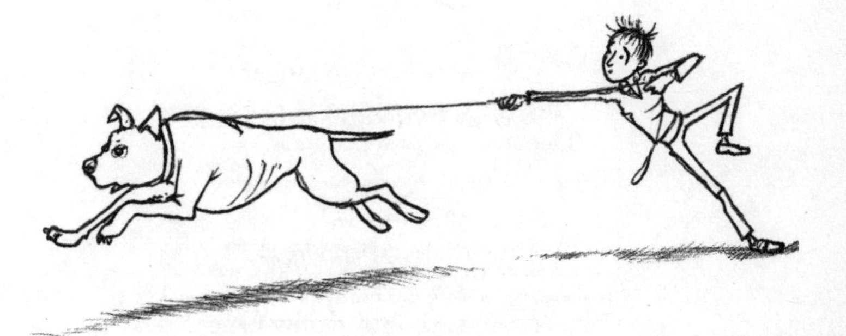

MICHAEL JOSEPH
an imprint of
PENGUIN BOOKS

MICHAEL JOSEPH

Published by the Penguin Group
Penguin Books Ltd, 80 Strand, London WC2R 0RL, England
Penguin Group (USA) Inc., 375 Hudson Street, New York, New York 10014, USA
Penguin Group (Canada), 90 Eglinton Avenue East, Suite 700, Toronto, Ontario, Canada M4P 2Y3 (a division of Pearson Penguin Canada Inc.)
Penguin Ireland, 25 St Stephen's Green, Dublin 2, Ireland
(a division of Penguin Books Ltd)
Penguin Group (Australia), 250 Camberwell Road,
Camberwell, Victoria 3124, Australia (a division of Pearson Australia Group Pty Ltd)
Penguin Books India Pvt Ltd, 11 Community Centre,
Panchsheel Park, New Delhi – 110 017, India
Penguin Group (NZ), 67 Apollo Drive, Rosedale, North Shore 0632, New Zealand
(a division of Pearson New Zealand Ltd)
Penguin Books (South Africa) (Pty) Ltd, 24 Sturdee Avenue,
Rosebank, Johannesburg 2196, South Africa

Penguin Books Ltd, Registered Offices: 80 Strand, London WC2R 0RL, England

www.penguin.com

First published 2009

3

Set in Adobe Caslon
Book design by Janette Revill
Printed in Great Britain by Clays Ltd, St Ives plc

A CIP catalogue record for this book is available from the British Library
ISBN: 978-0-718-15551-3

www.greenpenguin.co.uk

Penguin Books is committed to a sustainable future for our business, our readers and our planet. The book in your hands is made from paper certified by the Forest Stewardship Council.

For my mother and father,
my first and finest teachers

CONTENTS

☆ I ☆

A LOAD OF OLD TRIPE

I was christened James Joseph Johnson: James after my Granddad Greenwood and Joseph after my Grandpa Walker. My mum and dad call me Jimmy, my friends call me JJ, my granny calls me Jamie and my teacher calls me James. I don't really mind what people call me so long as they don't make fun of my name – which I am glad to say nobody does. I'm really grateful that my mum and dad didn't give me an unusual name like some of the boys in my class at school. There's Walter Wall and Percy Potter and Montgomery Smout, but the name I would hate, really really hate, would be Ignatius Plunket. Fancy going through life called Ignatius Plunket. It's funny but nobody ever teases Ignatius Plunket about his name. I suppose it's because Iggy (as we all call him) seems to be in a world of his own for most of the time, and he's such an easy-going, harmless, friendly sort of lad that everyone likes him. We also feel sorry for him, because he comes from a home none of us would want in a million years and he has horrible parents as well. But I'll tell you about Ignatius Plunket later on. I want to tell you a bit about myself first.

As I said, my name is Jimmy Johnson or JJ. I'm eleven years old, born just after the war in 1946. I don't have any brothers or sisters and I live with my mum (Brenda) and my dad (Colin) in a shiny red-brick terrace house with a greasy grey slate roof in Rotherton, South Yorkshire. I like where I live. There's not much room in our house, and we don't have a massive garden or a wonderful view, and sometimes the air has a sort of unpleasant metallic taste to it and bits of soot land on you like black snowflakes, but I wouldn't want to live anywhere else. The steelworks are near to where we live, and all that smoke and dust and dirt and grime gets blown on the air and seems to end up at the bottom of our street. Mum is always complaining that when she brings in the washing there are grubby marks and black smears on the clothes and she has to do them all over again.

Our house is at the very end of a long terrace, so we only have one neighbour, Mrs Sewell, who must be at least a hundred if she's a day and spends most of her life complaining about her various ailments and the state of the world. I'll tell you about her later on as well.

In our house Mum and Dad have the front bedroom and I have the one at the back. There's a boxroom, a living room, a small kitchen and the front room. We only go into the front room on very special occasions, such as when my Uncle Norman and Auntie Myra visit, and Mum keeps it really tidy. She's always in there dusting and polishing. There's her old upright piano, a heavy pale-green-coloured three-piece suite and a huge and ugly dark wooden buffet – a massive piece of furniture (Mum's pride and joy) with deep cupboards, open shelves and heavy drawers where all the crockery, cutlery and important documents are kept. I am not allowed to go into the front room without permission. The front door opens directly on to the street and at the back of the

house is a small yard with a high red-brick wall. There's an outside store, which at one time used to be the toilet, where Dad keeps his tools and I keep my bike. So that's where I live. Now I'll tell you about my parents.

My mum is thirty-three years old, and has long straight blonde hair, which she ties back in a pony-tail, and large blue eyes. She nearly died when I was born and was in hospital for two weeks on some sort of machine, and now she can't have any more children. Three days a week she works in the corner shop at the end of the street, so over the counter she gets to know everybody's business. She is one of these people who others like to confide in – a very good listener. She can also tell really interesting stories. Sometimes in the evening she shares some of the gossip with my dad or tells him about the customers who have been into the shop that day. I pretend not to listen, but I do. It's really good that she works in the corner shop because when a product goes beyond its sell-by date she is able to get it at a reduced price. Dad says that our larder is as well stocked as the shop where she works.

Dad is a bit older than Mum, and has bright ginger hair (which I have inherited) and a face full of freckles (which I have inherited too). Everyone says I am the spit and image of my dad. He was a despatch rider in the war

and there's a photograph of him on the piano in the front room. He's standing by a motorbike in his uniform with some of his pals, smiling like there's no tomorrow. Now he works as a de-seamer at the steelworks. His job is to hammer out all the faults in the steel when it has cooled down and been made into long strips. It's a really dirty and dangerous job but he never complains, even when he has to go out in the cold and dark on the night shift. Dad takes me to see Sheffield Wednesday play if they are at home, and on Sundays we often go fishing for perch and roach at Elsecar reservoir. He's great, my dad. He's taught me how to dribble a football, play cricket, bait a hook, ride a bike, fix a puncture, play the guitar and lots of other things as well. He rarely shouts and never hits me. The one thing I don't like about my dad is his singing. It's really embarrassing when he starts to sing on the banks of the reservoir or at the football match or when he's fixing something in the yard at the back. His favourite singer is someone called Alma Cogan, and when she sings she has a giggle in her voice. I hate it when my dad sings her songs and tries to do the giggle. I make myself scarce when he opens his mouth.

The only thing I don't like about my mum is that she always makes me eat what she puts on my plate at dinnertime. 'I can't be doing with fussy eaters,' she says, so I have to eat carrots (yuck) and sprouts (yuck) and mushrooms (yuck). 'If you had been a lad during the war,' she never tires of saying, wagging a finger in my direction, 'you'd have given your right arm for some fresh vegetables.' Fortunately she doesn't pile the plate high with this hated food, but I have to eat what she gives me or there's no pudding. I once devised a plan so I wouldn't have to eat the detested carrots. I filled my mouth with that horrible vegetable and pretended to cough into my handkerchief but spat out the contents of my mouth. Then I stuffed the handkerchief in my pocket and disposed of the carrots later by flushing them down the toilet. After the third occasion Mum got suspicious and put an end to my little ploy. She doesn't miss much, my mum.

Mum doesn't, thank goodness, make me eat some of the delicacies that my dad is fond of: black pudding (made from pigs' blood), pigs' trotters, liver, cowheel, polony (a fat sausage made of bacon, veal and pork suet) and chitterling (intestines of a pig). Dad's favourite meal is tripe. How he can eat the rubbery white lining of a cow's stomach I do not know, but he does and enjoys it. Mum cooks it in milk and drizzles chopped onions on the top. Of course, I can't be persuaded to try any.

'There are lots of people in the world, young man,' Mum says when she sees me screwing up my face at the sight of the pale rubbery slab of tripe bubbling in the pan, 'who would be only too pleased to have a plate of tripe and onions.' Then she says, 'If you had been a lad during the war, you'd have given your right arm for a piece.' Well, let them have it, I think to myself, I'd sooner eat stinging nettles. When Dad tucks into his tripe I watch fascinated as he devours the sickly white concoction and then licks his lips dramatically afterwards.

There is a tripe shop in Rotherton, and on Saturday morning, if I'm not out on my bike, I am sent to get a large piece of the white rubbery delicacy for Dad's tea. I never mind going to the shop because the owner is a most interesting woman. She has steely white hair, a round red face and large pink hands and stands behind her counter, arms folded, discussing the state of the world and the activities of the locals (some of whom 'are no better than they should be') with the regulars. I am quite content to wait and listen as she takes her time slicing piece after piece of tripe, weighing it ('It's just a bit over, love, is that all right?'), wrapping it in white greaseproof paper and all the while holding forth and entertaining her customers. I think people would be quite happy to go there for the conversation alone. I often enter the shop at some crucial part of a story: 'Of course if she'd have tied it up with a piece of string, it wouldn't have happened'; 'And I said to him, if you think I'm doing that with my bad back, you've got another think coming'; 'When the police finally arrived, do you know where she'd put it?' It's like story time at school.

One wet Saturday I was sent to buy Dad's tripe as usual and was coming out of the shop when I met my best pal, Michael Sidebottom. I call him Micky but not when his mum is around. My mum says that Mrs Sidebottom thinks she's a cut above everyone else, and when she comes into the corner shop for her 'special tea', which has to be ordered, she relates in a loud, posh, put-on voice, which everyone can hear, how well her husband is doing at work, how pleased the teachers at school are with Michael and all about the important people she has met. She also likes to tell people about the latest expensive appliance she's bought. The Sidebottoms were the first to get a television set, this small grey screen in a large wooden cabinet which has pride of place in her front room (which she calls 'the lounge'). I'd love a television set but Dad says they're too expensive and he'll get one when his numbers come up on the football pools.

Anyway, coming out of the tripe shop that Saturday

morning I met Micky. I was so busy talking to him about Sheffield Wednesday's chances against Bolton Wanderers at the match that afternoon that I didn't see the dog. It was a small wire-haired little terrier which must have smelled the tripe that I held in my hand. Before I knew it the mutt had jumped up, snatched the parcel out of my hand and run off. Micky and I gave chase, shouting and waving our arms in the air, and finally managed to corner the beast in an alley blocked by dustbins. It stood looking at us with the tripe dangling from its mouth. 'Drop!' ordered Micky in a loud assertive voice, pointing at the dog. 'Drop!' The dog continued to stare and then made a low growling noise. I grabbed the tripe and pulled, but the dog wouldn't let go, and tugged and shook it. Michael, whose mum had a fancy little poodle called Mimi, knew what to do. He picked up the terrier's back legs and amazingly it dropped the tripe, which I snatched up. Micky released the dog and it went mad, growling and jumping up and snapping and barking. Micky and I ran off with the dog at our heels.

'Sorry, love,' said the tripe shop owner, when I returned to the counter hoping for a replacement. 'I can't be doing that. You'll have to buy another piece.' I explained to her that I had no more money. 'Well, it will teach you to be more careful with your tripe, won't it?' she told me, before resuming a conversation with a customer about the state of the public urinals in the town centre.

Back home, I stared at the tripe. After all the tugging it was now twice the size and had been chewed. It had also picked up a fair bit of dirt. If I explained to Mum what had happened she would, no doubt, send me back to the shop, which was the last thing I wanted. I was keen to meet my pals at the park later that morning. So, before Mum could take the tripe from my hands, I shot up the stairs and into the bathroom.

'Have you got your dad's tripe?' came her voice up the stairs.

'Yes,' I shouted back, 'but I'm desperate for the toilet.' Then I washed the tripe thoroughly under the cold water tap.

Mum cooked the tripe, Dad ate it, and I watched with a screwed-up face.

'Delicious,' said Dad, licking his lips when he had finished. 'Best bit of tripe I've had in a long while. You must mention it, Brenda, the next time you go in the shop,' he continued. I gulped and prayed Mum would do no such thing.

☆ 2 ☆

BUTCH

At breakfast one Saturday morning, Dad sort of asked Mum casually, 'Do you remember Reg Turner, Brenda?'

'That little chap with the bald head and the arm full of tattoos?' replied Mum.

'Aye, that's the fellow,' said Dad. 'I used to work with him when I was on the furnaces.'

'Funny little man,' said Mum. 'He calls into the corner shop for his cigarettes but never passes the time of day. Just buys his twenty cigarettes, grunts a "thank you" and is out of the door like a cat with its tail on fire. Smokes like a chimney he does. He comes in with a fag in his mouth and lights up another when he's outside.' Mum looked daggers at me and stabbed the air with a finger. 'And don't you start smoking, young man. It's a mug's game.'

Dad winked at me, then turned his attention back to

Mum. 'He's just shy is Reg,' he told her. 'He's a nice man when you get to know him. I don't suppose he gets to meet many people living on his own.'

'You haven't invited him round for tea, have you?' asked Mum.

'No, no,' said Dad.

'Well, what about him?' she asked.

'He's to go into hospital next week for an operation.'

'No doubt all that smoking,' said Mum. 'It can't be doing his lungs any good at all with all those cigarettes he gets through.'

'Well, I don't know about that,' said Dad, 'but the thing is, he's got this dog.'

'I think I know what's coming,' said Mum, shaking her head, 'and the answer's "no".'

'We would only have to look after it for a week,' Dad told her, 'and Jimmy would help out, wouldn't you, son?'

'What, look after a dog?' I asked.

'Just for a few days,' said Dad. 'I mean, it's your half-term next week so you'll not be at school. You wouldn't mind looking after it, would you?' He looked at me expectantly and awaited my answer. I pretended to think about it, rubbing my chin and nodding. Deep down I was really keen. I would like nothing better than to look after a dog for a week, I thought, but I didn't want to look that eager. I had a plan, you see. 'You could take it to the fields and keep it out of your mum's way,' said Dad.

'Well,' I said, 'I could do, but I have a lot planned next week and the dog would take up a lot of my time. Now if you were to increase my pocket money?'

Dad sighed. 'That, young man, is blackmail.'

I smiled. 'Well, have we a deal?' I asked.

'OK,' he said. 'I'll double your allowance next week but you had better earn it.'

'Well,' said Mum, 'it seems that you two have decided

between you. Just you make sure, Jimmy, that you do look after the dog because you'll be responsible for it. I'm far too busy to be chasing around after it all week. You'll have to buy its food, feed it, take it for walks and clean up after it.'

'I will,' I said, trying not to sound too excited.

'Is it house-trained?' she asked Dad.

'Perfectly,' he replied.

'And docile?'

'Like a lamb.'

'And doesn't bark?'

'As quiet as a mouse.'

'And not big?'

'You could fit it in your shopping basket.'

'Mmmm,' hummed Mum. 'What's it called?'

'Butch,' Dad told her.

'Butch!' Mum repeated. 'It doesn't sound like a small, docile, house-trained dog to me.'

'Don't worry, Mum,' I said. 'I'll take good care of it. It'll be no problem.'

If only I had been right.

When Dad brought the dog home I couldn't believe it, I just couldn't believe it. I had always wanted a dog – a silky red-haired setter with doleful brown eyes or a cuddly corgi or a cute little chihuahua or a soft golden labrador or a frisky black and white collie or a long-haired spaniel. But Mum wouldn't let me have any pets. She said it would be cruel to keep an animal with her and Dad out at work and me at school all week, with no garden for it to exercise in and the street so busy with traffic. I would have settled for almost any kind of dog, even that miniature poodle that Micky's mum had, but I certainly didn't want a dog like Butch. He was like some prehistoric monster.

'Well, here we are,' said Dad sheepishly as he tried to pull this fat snarling creature through the front door. Eventually he managed to get the brute inside, and it was then that I stared in amazement.

There stood Butch, a big, ugly, barrel-bodied, bow-legged bull terrier with square pinky-white jowls and pale unfriendly eyes. The monster growled as it caught sight of me, showing a set of sharp teeth like tank traps, and stuck its fat tail in the air.

'I know what you're thinking, Brenda,' said Dad quickly when Mum emerged from the kitchen. Mum didn't say a word; she just stared in disbelief. 'I know it's not what you ...' His voice tailed off.

'It's horrible!' she cried. 'Colin, it will have to go back.

I am not having that brute in this house.'

'I can't take it back,' whined Dad. 'Reg is in hospital and there's nowhere to take it.' The dog growled and showed its set of sharp teeth again.

'It will have to go into those boarding kennels on Gilberthorpe Street,' said Mum. 'They look after animals while people are on holiday. You'll have to take it there.'

'Ah,' sighed Dad. 'There's a small problem with that. I did mention to Reg about the boarding kennels on Gilberthorpe Street when he asked me to look after Butch but he said he'd never settled there and, to be honest, I don't think they were very keen on having him back.'

'Colin!' said Mum sharply. 'We cannot look after that dog!'

'We can't just throw it out on the street,' pleaded Dad. 'And I did promise Reg we would look after it. It's just for a few days.' I could see by her expression that Mum was softening to the idea. 'I'm sure he's a very friendly dog, deep down,' said Dad, unconvincingly. 'We'll soon get to like him.'

'Well, just keep it out of my way,' said Mum, retreating to the kitchen and slamming the door behind her.

But Butch wasn't friendly and we didn't get to like him. He turned out to be bad-tempered and moody, and one hour after his arrival the entire bird population of the street migrated and even Mrs Sewell's tortoiseshell cat, the most vicious creature in the street, made itself scarce.

Butch soon made himself at home. On the first morning he sat on the pavement outside the front door, sunning himself and watching for any movement. I tied him to the street lamp with a piece of short rope and looked out of the window regularly to check on him. He seemed quite happy to sit there in the sun. I did notice that pedestrians began to cross the road when they caught sight of him, and later in the week they avoided the street altogether. Then people stopped calling. The milkman stopped collecting the bottles from outside the front door

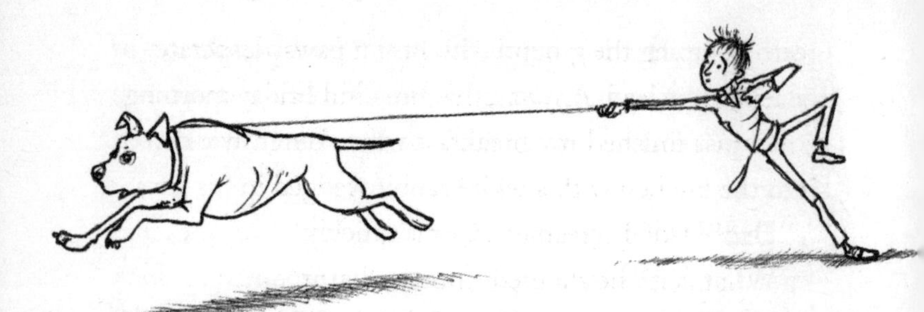

and posted a note through the letterbox to say the milk had to be collected from the depot in future, the postman posted our letters next door and asked for them to be passed on and the newspaper boy threw the paper over the back wall. Micky, my best friend, informed me that he would meet me at the park in future rather than call for me, provided I didn't bring the dog along. It wasn't so much me taking the dog for a walk, it was more the dog taking me for one, for it tugged me along the street growling and grunting and terrifying anybody who passed.

Then one morning when Dad was on the afternoon shift, the inevitable happened. Fortunately Mum was at work, so did not witness the crime. I knew Butch would kill something sooner or later. I told Dad that he would. I had seen the way he eyed anything that moved in the park and I had a real job holding him back when he saw other dogs. He snapped and snarled and gnashed his teeth, scraping the ground with his fat paws, desperate to be let off the lead. Anyway, that dreadful Friday morning I had just finished my breakfast when Butch wandered into the kitchen with a white rabbit wedged in his jaws.

'Dad! Dad!' I screamed. 'Come quickly.'

'What is it?' he shouted from the bathroom.

'Get down here now, Dad!' I shrieked. 'Now!'

I must have sounded pretty desperate, because I heard him a moment later bounding down the stairs.

'Whatever's the matter?' he shouted, rushing into the kitchen. He was half dressed and with his face covered in shaving cream.

'Look!' I cried. 'He's got a rabbit!'

'Oh my goodness!' gasped Dad when he caught sight of Butch standing staring up at him with the rabbit in his mouth.

'However did he get that?' cried Dad.

'I don't know,' I told him miserably. 'He must have slipped his rope. He just wandered into the kitchen with the rabbit in his mouth.'

Dad grabbed Butch by his collar. 'Drop!' he commanded. 'Drop!'

Butch looked up with the grey, watery, button eyes of a shark and tightened his grip on the rabbit.

'I said drop it!' shrieked Dad, his voice two octaves higher by this time. 'This instant!'

Butch made a rumbling noise like a distant train and continued to grip his victim.

'Do you hear me, you … you nasty, vicious, savage cur!' shouted Dad. 'Drop that rabbit!'

Butch blinked, then flopped down on the floor, still with his jaws tightly clamped together.

Dad attempted everything: trying to prise open the jaws with a hairbrush, tapping him on the head, dangling a morsel of juicy meat in front of his nose, nipping his nose to cut off his air, but nothing worked.

'There's nothing for it,' said Dad suddenly. 'We'll have to take him to the vet's.'

So we tugged and pulled Butch down the street, across the main road, past the shops, watched by amazed shoppers, still with the rabbit wedged in his mouth, until we arrived at the vet's.

The waiting room was crowded with people and their pets. They stared in shock and astonishment when we walked through the door. There was a man with a cage containing a noisy parrot which stopped squawking immediately at the sight of Butch, a nervous-looking woman with a sleepy white cat on her knee which soon woke up when it heard the growling, a little boy holding a hamster or some other small creature in a cardboard box, and a girl with a woolly-haired dog which whimpered pathetically when it caught sight of our canine companion. They all stared in horror, pets and owners, as Butch flopped on to the floor, tightening his grip on the rabbit, rumbling threateningly and eyeing everybody with those cold grey button eyes.

'Who's next?' asked the receptionist, popping her head round the door.

'He is!' they all chorused, pointing at Butch.

'It's the wolfish ancestry,' explained the vet cheerfully, surveying Butch as he stood bow-legged and brazen on his examination table. 'It's over ten thousand years, you know, since dogs were first domesticated but they still retain their wild instincts. We have modified a great many of their wild traits, of course, but all dogs still have that basic urge to kill. Even the most endearing of puppies is quite capable of savagery.'

'Much as I would like a potted history of the canine

world,' interrupted Dad, getting irritated, 'I do want to know what you can do about the rabbit.'

'Not much, I'm afraid. It's dead,' replied the vet flatly. 'It's been dead for hours. As soon as the dog grabbed it, the rabbit had no chance, no chance at all. Bull terriers have jaws like iron clamps. They lock on, you see. The rabbit's backbone would have been cracked like a nut.'

'Oh dear,' sighed Dad.

'The rabbit,' said the vet, 'is very definitely dead.'

'I know it's dead,' said Dad. 'I guessed it was dead as soon as I saw it. What are you going to do about it?'

'Well, I can't revive it, if that's what you are thinking,' the vet told him. 'I'm not a miracle worker.'

'I don't expect you to work miracles, Mr Fox,' said Dad. 'I just want the rabbit removed. The dog can't go through the rest of its life with a dead rabbit stuffed in its mouth!'

The vet agreed. He stroked Butch on his fat, round head and then tickled him behind his ears.

'He seems to like that,' said the vet, smiling.

Dad glowered.

A minute later Butch sort of yawned and the rabbit flopped out.

'There we are,' chortled the vet. 'You just have to know

the right spot.' He picked up the rabbit and examined it. 'Oh, this creature has been dead for hours, in fact it's beginning to smell.'

Having settled what Dad thought was an exorbitant bill for merely tickling a dog, we departed, taking with us the dead rabbit in a cardboard box.

'And not a word to your mother,' warned Dad on the way home.

I had a good idea who owned the rabbit. It belonged to the little girl who lived at the other end of the next street. I had seen her father sometimes on my way to school. He was a huge bear of man with a tangle of black curls and a sour expression. I wouldn't like to be the one who had to tell him about the rabbit, I thought, but I kept my thoughts to myself. Dad was upset enough as it was. The prospect of him getting a punch on the nose would only make matters worse.

'It's the Simmonite house at the end of the next street,' I told Dad. 'They kept the rabbit in a hutch in the back yard and the little girl would let it out sometimes for exercise. I've seen her do it when I've been coming back from school down the alley at the back of their house. Butch must have somehow got into the yard, killed it and brought it back here.'

'I don't know what I am going to say,' sighed Dad. 'I bet that rabbit meant the world to that little girl. She'll be heartbroken.'

'I'll come along to the house with you, Dad, and give you a bit of moral support,' I said. Perhaps if I was there, I thought, Mr Simmonite might not hit him.

'I just don't like the idea of telling her it was killed in such an awful way,' said Dad. 'Savaged to death by a dog.' We both looked at the dead rabbit in the card-board box. It looked pathetic, all floppy and lifeless, with its white fur speckled with blood and with dark, dirty streaks down its back.

'I think we ought to clean it up a bit before we take it back,' I suggested.

So we washed and cleaned the rabbit and dried it with Mum's hairdrier so it looked all white and fluffy – as it would have looked before Butch got a hold of it. Then we took it back.

There was no one at home, so Dad went round the back of the house and placed the dead rabbit gently back in its hutch.

'We'll call round later when they are in,' he explained, 'and tell them what happened. I guess the little girl will want some sort of burial. Perhaps her parents can tell her it died a natural death rather than being savaged to death by that brute on the pavement outside. Then I'll buy her another.'

We never did call at the house to explain what happened. When Mum arrived back from working in the corner shop that afternoon she was excited to tell us what she had heard over the counter. We sat at the kitchen table and never said a word.

'Well,' she began, 'you will never guess what somebody has gone and done at Mrs Simmonite's. When her husband got back from town this afternoon he found his little girl's rabbit dead in the hutch.'

'Oh dear,' said Dad looking straight at me.

'Evidently some person had put it there as some sort of sick joke,' said Mum.

'Sick joke?' Dad repeated.

'When the little Simmonite girl went out in the back yard early this morning to feed her pet rabbit,' continued Mum, 'she found it dead in the hutch.'

'Early this morning?' said Dad. 'Dead?'

'Colin,' said Mum, 'will you stop repeating what I say and listen. It's a very strange story. This morning the little Simmonite girl went out to feed her rabbit and found it dead in the hutch and as stiff as a post. According to her mother it was an old rabbit, couldn't see properly and had all sorts of ailments, and she said it was a blessing that it had died. Anyway, her father took the dead rabbit out of the hutch, put it in a plastic bag and placed it behind the dustbin ready to bury it later today. Then he took the little girl into town to get her another rabbit. When they got home you will never guess what they found?'

I knew exactly what they found but kept my mouth closed. 'What?' I asked innocently.

'Someone,' said Mum shaking her head, 'had taken

the dead rabbit, washed it and put it back in the hutch. Now who in their right mind would want to do such a horrible thing?'

'I've no idea,' I said, looking straight at Dad, who had gone a deep shade of red.

'I mean,' continued Mum, 'what sort of person would take a little girl's dead rabbit, wash it and clean it and put it back in the hutch? Mrs Simmonite said that her husband was furious and if he gets his hands on the joker who did it he'll be laughing on the other side of his face.' She looked at Dad. 'You're very quiet, Colin. Is something the matter?'

'No, no,' he said, trying to summon up a smile.

'And what's that dog been like today?' she asked.

'Butch?' he said. 'Oh, he's been as good as gold.'

~

☆ 3 ☆

IGNATIUS

Ignatius Plunket was an odd boy. That's what Mum used to say whenever she saw his long gangly figure meandering down the street, his head buried in a book. 'He's an odd boy, that Ignatius Plunket,' she would say. No one would disagree with her. Ignatius was certainly strange.

'He's more like a foundling orphan than one of the Plunket brood,' Mum would tell me every time she caught sight of Ignatius. 'Foundling', I later discovered, was an old-fashioned sort of word which described a child abandoned and left on the doorstep of some stranger's house because its parents couldn't or didn't want to care for the infant. 'I mean,' Mum would say, 'no one's telling me that that big fat lazy lump is his real father. Ignatius couldn't look more different if he tried.'

Mum had got a point. Mr Plunket was as round as a biscuit barrel, with a frizzy outcrop of dirty brown hair and a nose as big and heavy as a turnip. His fingers were as fat as pork sausages and he had small piggy ears and small piggy eyes. Dad said that during the war, Old Man Plunket got out of serving his King and country and made money on the black market while every other

able-bodied man was fighting. That's why he was so fat and well fed.

All the other five children in the Plunket family were the spit and image of their father, with their stocky build, large round noses and fuzz of mousy hair. Ignatius was the complete opposite. He was a tall scrawny boy with a sharp beak of a nose, ears like jug handles, large inquisitive eyes and a mop of jet black hair which fell like a curtain over his forehead. Whereas all the Plunkets had very red, healthy-looking faces, Ignatius's was as pale as the tripe Mum put in the pan when she was making Dad's favourite meal. I once heard Mum tell Dad that Mrs Plunket must have had a fling, as she called it, with an American GI just after the war.

Ignatius was different in other ways as well as in his appearance. For a start, he was really clever and spoke in this strange, grown-up, old-fashioned way.

'Mr and Mrs Plunket must have been at the back of the queue when they gave the brains out,' Mum would say when she saw them bustling around town, cigarettes dangling from their lips. 'They've not an ounce of sense between them. Thick as two short planks them two, and lazy as that dog we had to look after for Mr Turner.' But

their eldest son, Ignatius, had more brains than the rest of our class put together. He could add up quicker than our teacher, Mrs Sculthorpe, and knew more than her about history and geography and science. He was a better speller as well, and his stories and poems were as good as any in the books we studied at school. Some teachers would have found such a clever pupil a threat, but not Mrs Sculthorpe. If she didn't know the answer she would smile and say, 'Let's ask Ignatius.' Everyone knew she had a soft spot for Ignatius. Perhaps it was because he came to school in an old threadbare jumper, trousers a size too big with a shiny bottom, a coat a size too small and a shirt with frayed cuffs and collar. Perhaps it was because he was so good-natured and polite and never complained that Mrs Sculthorpe took a shine to him.

Whatever the reason, Ignatius would sit at the front desk watching the teacher like a hungry cat watches a goldfish in a bowl, devouring knowledge.

Looking as he did and acting as he did, you would have thought he would be an easy target for bullies, but that wasn't the case. Everyone left him alone, and Ignatius seemed to sail though life reading his books, not bothering anyone and smiling at the world.

On Monday mornings we would all line up at the teacher's desk with our dinner money. Ignatius was the only one in the class who didn't. We once asked him why he never paid anything like the rest of us, and he told us that his parents were on benefits because they were unemployed and short of money and that he got free school dinners. He had no problem with accepting the fact and was not at all ashamed or upset about it.

One day, as we made our way home from school, I asked him what was in the brown paper parcel stuffed underneath his arm. Ignatius announced, without any embarrassment, that Mrs Sculthorpe had given him some clothes that had once belonged to her son and were now too small for him. 'There's quite a nice jacket,' he told me cheerfully, 'and some rather sturdy shoes, hardly worn.'

Poor Ignatius never got to wear his new clothes. They were soon taken down to the market by his father and the proceeds ended up behind the bar at the Red Lion. 'Father said they were too good to wear,' he told me later without a trace of resentment, 'so he sold them.'

As I said, that was another thing about Ignatius – he didn't speak like a boy of eleven and certainly not like one who lived on our street. He used these old-fashioned phrases and fancy words and spoke with the sort of voice used by the snooty kids in the purple blazers, who went to the posh school at the other side of the town. Where this voice came from was another mystery, because all Mr and Mrs Plunket seemed to do was grunt and shout and swear.

On one bright sunny afternoon the school inspector called. Mrs Sculthorpe was as nervous as a rabbit cornered by a hungry fox. When she saw the tall dark figure striding down the corridor towards our classroom she gulped noisily, went white and gripped the edge of the desk to steady herself. The school inspector entered the room silently and crept to the back without a word. He sat in the corner, cross-legged, all through the lesson, scribbling away in his little black book with a face like one of those gargoyles you see spouting water on church roofs. When Mrs Sculthorpe had finished speaking and set us a story to write, he snapped the little black book shut, stood up and walked around the room looking at our work. He caught sight of Ignatius, at the front, staring out of the window with wide eyes, his mouth open.

'It appears someone is not concentrating upon his work,' the school inspector said, leaning over Ignatius and fixing him with his bright green eyes.

Any other pupil would have been terrified, but not Ignatius. He looked up sort of casually, smiled widely and without the least sign of nervousness replied cheerfully, 'Appearances can be deceptive.'

Two little red spots appeared on the school inspector's

pale cheeks. 'I beg your pardon?' he spluttered.

'It may appear to you that my mind is elsewhere,' said Ignatius. 'In fact I was considering what to write.'

'Perhaps you might like to tell me exactly what you were considering,' said the school inspector, scowling.

Mrs Sculthorpe looked like some statue at the front, completely still and lifeless and lost for words.

'Perhaps I might,' replied Ignatius.

'If you are asked a question, young man,' said the school inspector, clearly very irritated, 'I expect you to answer it.'

'Were you asking me a question?' asked Ignatius. 'It sounded rather like a statement to me. I take it you would like me to tell you what I am considering.'

'I would,' growled the school inspector with gritted teeth.

'I am considering what genre to use. Genre means the kind of writing. It's a French word, you know. I can't decide whether to write an adventure or a mystery story.'

'I know what the word genre means,' said the school inspector angrily. His face was now really red.

Mrs Sculthorpe suddenly got her voice back. 'Show the inspector your exercise book, please, Ignatius,' she said. There was a tremble in her voice.

Ignatius held up his book, which was snatched away from him by the visitor. The inspector flicked through the pages, then paused and examined a particular passage.

'Did you copy this?' he asked sharply, tapping the page with a long finger.

'No,' replied Ignatius. 'I wrote it.'

'Are you sure?'

'Of course I am sure,' sighed Ignatius. 'I would know whether or not I copied it, wouldn't I?'

'It's very good,' said the school inspector. It didn't sound like a compliment but Ignatius took it as one.

'Oh, thank you,' he said, brushing a curtain of hair from his forehead.

The school inspector scrutinized Ignatius for a moment, taking in the shabby clothes and the pale, rather unhealthy-looking white face. I could see what he was thinking: 'Appearances can indeed be deceptive.'

*

'Would you like to ask Ignatius round for tea one day next week?' Mum asked me one Saturday.

'I could do,' I replied.

'I don't suppose he gets asked round to people's houses very often,' she said.

'I should think never,' I replied.

'It'll be a little treat for him,' said Mum. 'I can't imagine he gets many treats in that house.'

So, the following Monday after school, Ignatius arrived at the door for his tea.

'Thank you very much for inviting me, Mrs Johnson,' he said to Mum. 'It is very kind of you. I don't get out a lot, you know.'

'It's a pleasure, Ignatius,' replied Mum. 'Would you like to wash your hands before we sit down at the table?'

'Thank you,' he said. 'I would.'

'Jimmy, show your friend where the bathroom is,' said Mum. I took Ignatius upstairs, showed him where the bathroom was and returned to help Mum set the table.

Ignatius was ages in the bathroom. We could hear him splashing and gargling and flushing and then he started to whistle.

'Go and see what he's doing,' said Mum. 'He's been in there for ten minutes or more.' When he finally emerged from the bathroom, Ignatius looked as if he had had a bath. His face shone where he had scrubbed it, his hair was wet and he smelled of perfumed soap.

'Indoor toilet. Hot water,' he sighed. 'What a treat. We only have the outside lavatory and cold water at home. And you have proper toilet paper and towels too.'

'Do you want to see my room?' I asked him.

'I would,' he said, following me into my bedroom. 'It must be nice having your own room. I sometimes wish I had a room to myself. My brothers and sisters do tend to be rather noisy and, of course, I have to turn the light off just when I get to an exciting part in my book.' He picked up my alarm clock and examined it, glanced at the football posters on my wall, looked at the model aeroplanes on the window-sill and peered out of

the window. 'Oh, you can see the cemetery from here,' he said brightly, as if it was a spectacular view over open countryside. He wandered out on to the landing and into Mum and Dad's room.

'Best not go in there,' I whispered.

'I'm just having a little peek,' he said, stepping through the door. 'I won't touch anything.' He looked around as if he was in a museum examining the exhibits. 'This is very nice,' he murmured, 'very nice indeed.' He ran a long finger along Mum's dressing-table. 'Lovely piece of furniture.'

I was getting a bit nervous now. Mum didn't like me going into her room, never mind a stranger. 'Come on,' I said. 'Tea will be ready.'

'I hope you like cottage pie, Ignatius,' said Mum when she saw us coming down the stairs.

'I can't say that I have ever had any, Mrs Johnson,' he told her, 'but it sounds delicious.'

Cottage pie was one of Mum's specialities: succulent minced beef swimming in thick rich gravy and covered in a mound of fluffy potato. Mum and I watched fascinated as Ignatius tucked in, his knife and fork moving with such speed that he had cleaned his plate before we had hardly begun.

'Another helping, Ignatius?' said Mum.

'That would be splendid, Mrs Johnson,' he said. 'This is delicious, and the carrots were done to a turn.' Mum gave me a look.

When he saw Mum bring the steaming tin of rice pudding in from the kitchen, Ignatius sniffed the air, sighed and said, 'Rice pudding, home made, my very favourite.' He had second helpings of that as well. Then he leaned back on the chair and patted his stomach. 'TTT,' he said, smiling.

'I'm sorry?' said Mum.

'Tummy touching table,' he explained. 'I read it once in a book. Sherlock Holmes, I think. That was truly a banquet, Mrs Johnson. The very best meal I have ever had.'

Mum gave a great smile. I could see she was very pleased with the compliment. 'Thank you very much, Ignatius. It's nice to be appreciated.' She gave me a sideways glance. 'You must come again.'

'I would like that very much,' he replied. 'I am afraid that I can't return the invitation and ask James to come for tea at my house. My mother is not a good cook and hasn't been all that well lately.' I was glad of that, I thought to myself. The very last thing I wanted was tea in the Plunkets' house. 'Would you like me to help with the washing up?' he asked Mum.

'No, no,' she said. 'That's Jimmy's little job.'

'I don't mind at all,' he said. 'In fact I would quite enjoy it.'

'Really, you don't need to bother,' said Mum. 'But it was kind of you to ask.'

Ignatius stood and tucked the chair under the table. 'Well, I had better make tracks,' he said. 'I do have to help with the chores. I have some washing to do this evening. My mother has a skin condition – eczema, you know – and water does tend to irritate her. She can't wash clothes.'

'Of course,' said Mum, giving me a knowing look. I could see what she was thinking. The only condition Ignatius's mum had was idleitis. 'Well, it's been nice having you round.'

'Thank you very much, Mrs Johnson,' said Ignatius, giving a little bow. 'I'll see you tomorrow at school, James.' Then he strode for the door.

When the door had closed behind him, Mum started to shake her head and chuckle.

'What's amusing you?' I asked.

'He's an odd boy that Ignatius Plunket,' she said, 'a very odd boy.'

It was about an hour later that Mum came into my bedroom. I was just finishing gluing a model Spitfire and had just the wheels to stick on.

'Have you seen my locket?' she asked.

'No.'

'Are you sure?'

'Sure.'

'It was on the dressing-table in my bedroom.'

'I've not seen it.'

'Well, that's very strange,' said Mum. 'I'm certain I put it there when I came in from work.'

'Have you looked in the bathroom?' I asked.

'I've looked everywhere,' she told me.

'Well, I haven't seen it,' I said. 'Don't worry. It'll turn up.'

'It belonged to your Granny Greenwood, that locket. Gold it was, with a picture of your granddad inside. Now where could it be?' Mum was just about to go out when she stopped and looked puzzled. 'Ignatius Plunket didn't go into my bedroom, did he?'

My heart sank. 'No,' I mumbled.

'Are you sure? He was upstairs an awful long time.'

'Sure,' I said. My answer didn't sound very convincing, because Mum came over, sat on my bed and looked me hard in the face.

'He did, didn't he? He went in my bedroom.'

'Only for a minute,' I said, 'and I was with him. He won't have taken your locket.'

'What was he doing in my bedroom?' she demanded.

'He was just looking. He didn't touch anything,' I told her.

'Oh no, not half,' said Mum, standing up and folding her arms tightly across her chest. 'That gold locket was there when I got in from work and now it's gone, so who do you think took it, the fairies?'

'You might have put it somewhere else,' I said feebly.

'Of course I didn't!' snapped Mum. 'I remember putting it on my dressing-table when I came in from work and it's been stolen and we know who took it.' She took a great heaving breath. 'You ask him round for tea, he comes into your home, has helping after helping and sits there as if butter wouldn't melt in his mouth, as polite as can be, and all the time he's a little thief. Can't keep his grubby little fingers off other people's things. That's all the gratitude you get for feeling sorry for him. Well, he's not getting away with it.'

'What are you going to do?' I asked with a sinking feeling in the pit of my stomach. I guessed what Mum was going to do. I really didn't need to ask.

'I'm going to get it back, that's what,' said Mum. 'I'm going along to the Plunkets to get my locket back. It was given to your granny by your granddad and she gave it to me. I wear it all the time. It has sentimental value and if that boy thinks ... '

'Please don't!' I cried. 'Please don't go round to his house.'

'Don't be so silly!' she exclaimed. 'You don't seriously think I'm going to forget all about it, do you, let him get away with it?'

'Can we have another look?' I pleaded. 'I'll help you.'

'I've done all the looking I'm going to do,' she told me angrily. 'I remember distinctly putting it on my dressing-table. I'm going round to the Plunkets to get it back.'

'Let me go,' I begged her. 'Let me get it back.'

'No,' Mum said sharply. 'It takes an adult to sort this out

and I intend to give those Plunkets a piece of my mind. Nobody in the street likes them. Neither of that boy's parents has done a day's work in their lives, scrounging and living off others. Anything free and they're the first in the queue. They give the street a bad name. Dirty steps, rotten window-frames, unpainted door, filthy windows and garden like a jungle. Now they've taken to thieving.'

'Please! Please, Mum!' I begged again, my eyes filling with tears. 'Please, let me get it back.'

Mum calmed down a bit and thought for a moment. 'You've got five minutes, young man, five minutes, and if that locket is not in my hand by then, I'm coming round to get it.'

I scurried out of my room, dropping the model aeroplane in the process, scrambled down the stairs and out through the front door and down the road until I arrived outside the dirty unpainted door of the Plunkets. I thanked my lucky stars when Ignatius answered the door. He was wearing an old frayed apron.

'Oh, hello,' he said cheerfully.

'Hello, Iggy,' I said, wondering what I was going to say next.

'I'm afraid you can't come in. The house is a bit crowded at the minute and I'm in the middle of washing.'

'Ignatius … Iggy …' I started.

'Yes?'

I gulped. 'When you were round at my house, did you see a locket on my mum's dressing-table?'

'No,' he replied simply.

'When we went in her room, you remember, well, did you see a gold locket on the dressing-table?'

'I didn't,' he said.

'It's just that Mum's lost it and she's in a real state about it. It belonged to my granny. She remembers putting it on the dressing-table when she came in from work and it's not there now.'

Ignatius thought for a moment. He ran a hand through his mop of dusty hair and wrinkled his forehead into a frown. 'Does your mother think I took it?' he asked.

'No, of course not,' I lied, feeling my face becoming hot.

'That I stole it?'

'No, no, it's just that we can't find it. She wonders if you might have seen it.'

'She does think I stole it, doesn't she?' he said. He didn't sound angry or upset, just matter-of-fact.

'Well … yes, she does,' I said, looking at my shoes and feeling awful.

Ignatius undid the apron and folded it carefully as if it were a piece of precious cloth. 'I'll only be a moment!' he shouted to some unseen presence inside the house. 'I'll come along and have a word with her,' he told me. 'Sort the matter out. I'm sure there's a simple explanation.'

We met Mum running down the road. I wanted the ground to open up and swallow me. I was embarrassed and ashamed and scared. My stomach tightened.

'Ignatius!' Mum panted.

'Mrs Johnson,' he said as she rushed up to him. 'I didn't take your locket. I wouldn't do such a thing.' There was no defiance blazing in his eyes.

Mum was trying to get her breath. 'Ignatius,' she began again.

'I'm not a thief, Mrs Johnson. I wouldn't repay your kind hospitality by stealing from you.' He didn't sound angry or offended. His voice was as usual, calm and friendly.

'I know,' said Mum, at last beginning to breathe more easily. 'I know you are not a thief. I found the locket.'

'You did!' I cried.

'It was on the floor behind the dresser,' Mum told us rather shamefaced. 'It must have slipped off. I found it just this minute.'

'Well, that's all sorted out then, hasn't it?' said Ignatius, smiling. He just stood there as calm as anything.

'Yes it has,' said Mum, her eyes refusing to meet his. 'I just wanted to tell you and to say …' Mum took a deep breath before continuing in a quavery voice, 'that I'm sorry, Ignatius, for thinking you had taken it.'

'That's all right, Mrs Johnson,' he said, his gaze settling upon her. 'It's quite understandable. All's well that ends well.'

Mum stood there for a moment. I could see she wanted to say something else but she was lost for words. 'Well, I'll get back, then,' she said, and walked off leaving us together on the pavement.

'I'm sorry,' I said quietly. 'I'm really sorry, Iggy, about all that.'

'Nothing to be sorry about,' he said casually. 'It's not your fault.'

'My mum should never have thought you had taken it,' I said.

'It was a natural reaction,' he said, giving a small shrug. 'Adults often jump to the wrong conclusions where children are concerned. Your mum's all right. Adults rarely apologize. They like to be right. She said she was sorry, so let's forget it ever happened.'

'Yes,' I said, smiling. 'Let's forget it.'

Then Ignatius looked at me straight in the eyes. 'You didn't think I took your mother's locket, did you?' he asked. His stare made me feel really uncomfortable.

'Of course not,' I lied. 'Of course not.'

~

☆ 4 ☆

THE BOWL

'Do I have to do it this Saturday morning?' I moaned.

'Yes, you do,' said Mum. She was busy ironing in the living room.

'Can't I do it next Saturday?' I asked.

'No.'

'Please?'

'No!' Mum snapped, banging down the iron. 'I want you to go through all your cupboards and drawers in that tip of a bedroom of yours today and clear out all those old toys and books and any clothes you don't wear any more.'

I gave a great heaving sigh.

'And less of the sound effects,' said Mum. 'Go on, up to your room and get cracking.'

I had brought home a letter the day before from Mr Morgan, saying that there was to be the annual fund-raising event at the school the following Saturday and asking parents to send in items to sell.

To raise money, every year the school opens on a Saturday for the bring-and-buy sale. It's really a sort of jumble sale, and the hall gets full to bursting with stalls selling toys, books, clothes, games, food, bottles, sports equipment, crockery and old pots, bric-a-brac, plants, and all sorts of things that people don't want any more. Mum and Dad always go along to man one of the stalls and I get roped in to help. I don't mind being on a stall, in fact I quite enjoy it. For a start the stallholders get to see what's for sale before the doors open to the public, and you can pick up some really good bargains before everyone else. One year I got a complete set of lead soldiers and another year a nearly new tennis racket. I also like being on the stall and trying to get buyers to pay more for an item. Dad says I'd make a really good market trader the way I shout and barter. What I don't like, however, is that every year I have to go through the things in my bedroom, which I find a real chore, particularly on a sunny Saturday morning when I could be down at the park playing football with Barry and Kevin.

'It's a really good opportunity,' said Mum, folding up one of my dad's shirts, 'to have a good old clear-out.'

'But not this morning,' I groaned.

'Yes, this morning,' she said, 'and no arguments.'

'But ...'

'No buts,' she interrupted. 'And if you don't sort out all your things this morning, then I will, and you wouldn't be best pleased if I was to decide what to keep and what to give away, now would you?'

'No, I wouldn't!' I exclaimed.

'Well then,' said Mum. 'Off you go. Your dad's put two cardboard boxes on the landing for all the things you no longer want and he'll help you take them to school on Monday.'

I started sorting through my possessions in a really bad mood, but by the end of the morning I was in a much better frame of mind. I discovered things I had not seen for years, games I had never played, books I had never read, stamps I had never stuck in my album, and the real find – a money-box full of coins that I had forgotten about. By lunchtime the two cardboard boxes on the landing were bursting.

'All done,' I told Mum, feeling pretty pleased with myself.

'That's a good lad,' she said. 'Now, what are your plans for the rest of the day?'

Sheffield Wednesday was playing an away game down south that afternoon, so Dad and me were not going to the match.

'Can I ride over to Barry's on my bike?' I asked her.

'I should think so, if you're careful on the road.'

'And don't talk to strangers,' I added before she could mention it, 'and be back before it gets dark.'

'Before you go,' she said, 'you've got time to pop into Mrs Sewell's with her shopping.' Mum did our next-door neighbour's shopping every Friday.

'Aw, Mum,' I moaned.

'Never you mind the "Aw, Mum." It's only next door and she'll be waiting for it. I'd take it myself, but I've got all this ironing to finish and then I want to blitz your bedroom now I can see the carpet. You know how she talks. I'd never get away.'

'I hate going next door with her shopping,' I said. 'All she does is moan and groan and complain. She's a pain in the neck.'

'That's because she's lonely. She's glad of a bit of company, although she'll never admit it. You'll be old one day, young man. Now go on, her shopping's in the kitchen.'

Mrs Sewell had lived in the house next door for as long as I could remember. Dad describes her as a bad-tempered old stick and he's right. She likes nothing better than moaning about her many ailments and complaining about everything and anybody. Mum says she feels sorry for her because she never goes out and no one, except us and the doctor, ever visits her, and that it's no wonder she's grumpy and annoying.

I hate going next door. Mrs Sewell's house is dark and dusty and smells like the hamster cage at school. Mrs Sewell smells as well – of mothballs and old age – and she wears old cardigans that are thin and tattered and thick black skirts with stains down the front and dirty brown slippers with holes in the toes. Dad says it's not as if she can't afford to buy new clothes, because her husband, long since dead, worked for years in the Council Offices and must have been on a good salary. It's just that she's mean and doesn't like spending anything. The old lady never throws anything out in case, as she says, 'it may come in handy', so her living room is a cluttered mass of all sorts of useless items. She saves bottles and bags and old cardboard boxes, jam jars and bits of string and rubber bands, plastic margarine tubs and old newspapers. Her house is like a junk shop. She could have her own bring-and-buy sale, although I guess nobody would want most of her stuff. But it's not just the smelly old house that I don't like. It's the cat. Mrs Sewell has this vicious tomcat called Tibby, a big fat tortoiseshell beast more tiger than cat that spits and hisses and scratches as soon as I get in the door. Once it climbed up the threadbare curtains and leapt on to my shoulders and scratched my face before I could sweep it off. 'It's only being playful,' said Mrs Sewell, as the cat shot out of the door hissing. 'I hope you've not hurt him.'

Anyway, I hate going round to her house so Mum usually delivers the shopping.

That Saturday I banged really loudly on the front door and then, a moment later, I heard a rattling of chains and a scraping of bolts. The door opened a fraction and a wrinkled screwed-up old face peered through the crack.

'Who is it?'

'It's me, Mrs Sewell,' I said.

'Who?'

'Me. Jimmy from next door.'

'What do you want?'

'I've got your shopping.'

'What?'

'Shopping!' I shouted. 'I've come with your shopping.'

She opened the door and examined me like some specimen in a museum case. 'You had better come in,'

she said. 'And wipe your feet. I don't want you traipsing in with dirt on your shoes and marking the carpet.'

That's a laugh, I thought. The pavement outside was cleaner than her carpet.

'I won't come in,' I said. 'I'll just leave your shopping in the hall.'

She ignored me. 'Bring it through to the kitchen.'

'Can I leave it here?' I asked.

'And how am I supposed to carry that little lot with my bad back?' she said quickly and irritably. 'Bring it through and do as you're told.'

So I carried the bag of groceries into her kitchen, holding my breath as I entered the house. 'Where shall I put it?' I asked, looking around for an empty space amidst the clutter.

'Put it by the table,' she ordered.

I did as I was told and headed for the front door. 'I'll be off then,' I said.

'Wait a minute! Wait a minute; I've got something for you.'

Gosh, I thought, this is a new one. I'm going to get a tip. She was actually going to give me something for bringing her shopping.

She shuffled over to the sink and pulled out a drawer

and began rummaging among the cutlery. Then she held up an old rusty tin-opener which she thrust into my hands. 'Ask your dad to have a look at this,' she said. 'It won't work. You can bring it round later on.'

I felt like saying: 'Is there anything else, Mrs Sewell? Would you like him to redecorate your house, put in a shower, carpet the living room, build a conservatory?' But I stuffed the tin-opener in my jeans pocket and left.

'And don't let the cat out!' she shouted after me as I slammed the front door. Dad fixed the tin-opener and I was instructed to make a return visit.

There was no way I was going back into that smelly house, so I decided to post the tin-opener through the letterbox. I lifted up the flap really quietly and fed it through. It was as if the door was on some sort of spring, because as soon as the tin-opener hit the floor in Mrs Sewell's hallway, the door swung open.

'What are you doing?' she demanded.

'Returning your tin-opener,' I told her. 'My dad's fixed it for you. I posted it through your letterbox.'

'Well, I can't bend down with my bad legs,' she said. 'Pick it up and bring it into the kitchen.'

Mrs Sewell wouldn't let me leave until she had tried the tin-opener to see if it worked. The killer cat was there, sitting on the top of a cupboard watching me with green eyes and hissing menacingly. I moved well away from it.

'It doesn't work as well as it used to,' she complained.

'You ought to get yourself a new one then,' I said.

'I don't need a new one,' she told me. 'It'll have to do.' The cat meowed. 'He's not happy,' she told me.

'Who?' I asked.

'Tibby. He's cut his tongue on that.' She pointed to an old blue bowl on the table. 'It's got a crack in it and it's all rough round the rim. He must have caught his tongue on it when he was licking up his milk. I shall have to get him a new bowl. You can ask your mum to get me one. Plastic, not expensive. You can get rid of that old bowl for me.'

Crikey, I thought, she is actually going to throw something out. 'Are you sure it won't come in?' I asked her mischievously.

'No,' she said. 'I don't want Tibby cutting his tongue again. Anyway, I've never liked that bowl. My sister gave it to me. She was probably given it and didn't like it so she passed it on to me. Chuck it away.'

I wondered to myself if the words 'please' and 'thank you' had ever been part of her vocabulary.

Well, I didn't chuck the bowl away. I scrubbed it and polished it and took it to the bring-and-buy sale the following Saturday. It looked pretty good in the centre of the table, a pale blue with delicate flowers decorating the side.

'I'd have that,' said Mum, 'if it wasn't for the damage. Perhaps nobody will notice that crack. Perhaps we'll get a couple of pounds for it.'

We did a good trade on our stall but the bowl remained unsold. Lots of people picked it up but when they saw the damage shook their heads and returned it to the table. When things quietened down a bit Mum went to get a cup of coffee and Dad to help on another stall, so I was left alone. That's when I saw Ignatius wandering around aimlessly with his hands in the pockets of the old baggy trousers he wore for school.

'Hello, Iggy,' I said, as he passed my stall.

'Oh, hello, James,' he said. 'I didn't see you there. I'm just having a little wander around, not that I'm going to buy anything. Mum and Dad might pop in later. They have business in town this morning.' More likely in the pub, I thought. He began looking through all the bric-a-brac on the table, picking up an object and examining it closely like an expert at an auction. He spent quite some time looking at the bowl. 'This is interesting,' he said.

'I think it's Chinese.' He replaced it in the centre of the table at the very moment when this large, red-cheeked man approached. He glanced at the items on the table and then his eyes settled on the bowl. He picked it up and turned it around in his hands, inspecting it closely and thoroughly.

'How much for this?' he asked.

Before I could answer, Ignatius asked him, 'How much are you prepared to pay?'

'Couple of quid.'

'It's worth more than that,' said Ignatius, taking the bowl from him.

The man laughed. 'What, an old pot bowl with a crack in it?'

'Actually, it's not pot,' Ignatius told him. 'It's porcelain.'

'Get away,' said the man. 'Cheap pottery. Anyway, what would a kid like you know about china?'

'So it is porcelain china then,' said Ignatius, still holding on to the bowl, 'and not an old pot bowl?'

'It might be,' said the man, observing him suspiciously.

'You can always tell china,' said Ignatius, tapping the bowl with a long finger. 'It makes a little chinging sound. I read that in a book.'

'Well, I'm not paying more than a fiver,' said the man.

'Then someone else will be the lucky owner,' Ignatius told him.

The man thought for a moment. 'Ten quid, then.'

'This rare and lovely Chinese ceramic bowl is worth a lot more than ten pounds. It could be very rare.'

'And it could be a load of rubbish,' said the man, walking away.

'What was that all about?' I asked. 'We could have got ten pounds for that old pot.'

'He'll be back,' said Ignatius, smiling. 'I could see it in that man's eyes that he wanted it and knew what it was. I've seen him before, you know. He has an antique stall down on the market. You mark my words, he'll be back.' With that he placed the bowl back in the centre of the table.

Five minutes later, as Iggy had predicted, the man returned. He placed five ten pound notes on the table.

'That's my last offer,' he said. 'Take it or leave it.'

'Were you to add another ten pounds,' said Iggy, 'I'd take it.'

'You ought to be down the market, you kid,' growled the man, reaching into his pocket for his wallet. 'You'd make a ruddy fortune.' He slapped down two crumpled five pound notes.

'Would you like it wrapping up?' asked Ignatius pleasantly.

'No,' scowled the man and strode off clutching the bowl.

Mum made me take half the money round to Mrs Sewell. She said it was only fair, bearing in mind the value of the bowl. The old lady counted the money with remarkable speed considering her arthritic fingers.

'You perhaps could have got more for it,' she said. 'It might have been one of these Ming bowls and worth thousands.'

'You told me to chuck it out,' I said. The mean old biddy, I thought. If it had been up to me I'd have kept the money. 'You told me you never liked it and you didn't know what it was. Anyway, if it hadn't been for Ignatius

Plunket I would have sold it for a pound.'

'Family of ne'er-do-wells, the Plunkets,' she said. 'Father's never done a day's work in his life.'

'Yes, well, Ignatius is different,' I told her. I was angry now. 'He's my friend and he's not a ne'er-do-well, whatever one of those is. It was Ignatius who knew the bowl's value and you should be grateful.'

'Huh,' she grunted. 'Have you finished?'

'No I haven't,' I told her boldly. 'Any other person would have given him a reward.'

'Reward!' she spluttered, as if I had said a rude word.

'Yes, Mrs Sewell,' I said, 'a reward. You are thirty pounds better off because of him and all you do is complain that you could have got more.'

She looked at me, screwing her eyes up, and then she gave a little smile. 'You're a one, aren't you? Got a temper on you, I can see that, and you're not frightened to speak your mind. Like my husband was, you are. He used to say things as they were. Always spoke his mind. Got him into trouble at the Council Offices on more than one occasion.' She plucked the two crumpled five pound notes from the envelope. 'Take that,' she said, 'and give half to that Plunket boy and keep the rest for yourself.'

I didn't know what to say. I just stared at the money.

'Well, go on, take it,' she said, pushing the notes into my hand, 'before I change my mind.'

'Thank you, Mrs Sewell,' I said. 'That's very generous of you.'

'And you can come and see me again,' she said almost grudgingly. 'That's if you have a mind to do so. Oh, and when you get home tell your father that the tin-opener he was supposed to have mended doesn't work.'

~

☆ 5 ☆

THE LAST LAUGH

Mrs Sculthorpe gave one of her famous smiles. It stretched from ear to ear like the grinning frog in the tank on the nature table. When she stopped smiling we expected to see lipstick on her ears. Next to her was a pale, blond-haired boy with blue eyes.

'Will you all look this way, please,' said Mrs Sculthorpe. 'And that includes you, Michael Sidebottom. Thank you. Now, this morning we have a new addition to our class.' She turned in the direction of the new boy and her smile seemed to stretch even wider. 'This is Jean-Paul. He doesn't speak very much English because he's from another country, so you will all have to speak slowly for him to understand you. Now Jean-Paul is only with us for a couple of weeks but during that time I am sure you will all make him feel at home.'

'Where's he from, miss?' asked Valerie Harper, her hand waving like a daffodil in the wind.

'I'm just about to tell you, Valerie dear, if you'll let me finish,' said the teacher sharply.

The new boy stared around the room with a blank expression on his face. If I'd been up there in front of the whole class with all those eyes on me I'd have been bright red. But he just stood there as calm as anything. I don't suppose he understood a word Mrs Sculthorpe was saying.

'Can anyone guess which country Jean-Paul comes from? His name should give you a clue.'

'Is he from Wales, miss?' asked Valerie Harper.

'No, he's not from Wales,' replied Mrs Sculthorpe.

'Is he from Ireland, miss?' asked Kevin Murphy. 'My cousin's from Ireland and she's got a funny name. My dad says my Uncle Sean wants his head examining calling her that.'

'Jean-Paul is not a funny name, Kevin. In fact it's quite a common name in his country.'

'Miss, my cousin's name is Attracta,' Kevin Murphy went on.

'Blimey!' Barry Bannister piped up. 'Fancy calling somebody a tractor! What's her brother called – a combine harvester?'

'No!' spluttered Kevin. 'Not a tractor like the one you drive around a farm. It's all one word – Attracta.'

'That will do, Kevin. Now Jean-Paul is not from Ireland. People from Ireland speak English.'

'Miss,' persisted Kevin, 'that's not what my dad says. He says he can't understand a word they say when we visit my Auntie Monica in Dublin.'

'Thank you very much, Kevin. I think we've heard quite enough about your Irish relations.' Mrs Sculthorpe looked around the class. I just knew what she would say next. 'Shall we ask Ignatius?' she said.

Ignatius Plunket rubbed his chin and swept the curtain of dusty brown hair from his forehead. 'Jean-Paul could be from France,' he said, 'and then again he could be from Belgium. There is a possibility he's from Switzerland, although most people there speak German, or he might be from Luxembourg or Monaco.'

'Well, you were right first time, Ignatius,' Mrs Sculthorpe told him. 'Jean-Paul is from France.'

The teacher turned to the new boy and did an imitation of a frog again.

'There's an empty place next to James Johnson there,' she said really slowly and pointing to the seat next to mine. 'You'll look after Jean-Paul for today, won't you, James?'

'Yes, miss,' I replied.

'And remember, he doesn't speak much English so you will have to point to things and speak slowly.'

Then the French boy spoke. 'I understand very much what you are saying. I learn to speak Engleesh in my school in France.'

'Well,' said Mrs Sculthorpe, 'that will make things a whole lot easier, Jean-Paul.'

'In my school in France, I learn to speak Engleesh with Madame Poisson. I learn it for two years.'

'And you speak it very well, too,' said Mrs Sculthorpe. 'Now you sit next to James and he'll tell you all about our school.'

'What's your second name?' I asked Jean-Paul when he had taken his seat next to mine.

'Please?'

'Your other name. Jean-Paul what?'

'Jean-Paul Savigny-Richeux.'

'Crikey! That's a mouthful,' I laughed.

'What is this mouthful?'

'You know – a lot to say. Bit like James Joseph Johnson really. That's my full name.'

'Ah, *oui*.'

'Whereabouts in France are you from?'

'Do you know France?' he asked.

'No,' I replied. 'Never been out of England.'

'Then you would not know where I live.'

'I might,' said Ignatius, who had been listening to our conversation.

Ignatius in his old threadbare jumper, trousers a size too big and shirt with its frayed cuffs and collar must have looked very strange to the French boy.

'It is much bigger than your town,' said the boy. 'It is called Le Havre.'

'I know where that is,' said Ignatius in a really friendly voice. 'There was a lot of action there during the war. It's a very important port, Le Havre. It was very heavily bombed. I read this very interesting book about submarines and –'

The French boy cut him off. 'It is much warmer in Le Havre. It does not rain with all zer winds and it ees not cold.'

'Oh, it's all right here in summer, isn't it, Iggy?' I said.

'Yes,' Ignatius began, 'it gets –'

'I am also not liking the *mauvaise odeur*.'

'The what?' I asked.

He made a sniffing noise.

'I think he means the smell,' said Ignatius.

'Oh, the stink,' I said. 'You get used to that after a bit. It's from the knacker's yard.'

'*Pardon?*' The boy's forehead furrowed. He looked very puzzled.

'The knacker's yard,' I explained. 'They get loads of old bones and boil them up to make glue. If the wind's in the wrong direction there's a right pong. Course, it could be the sewage works on Midden Road or Demoulders Tannery on Common Lane.'

'They eat horses in France, don't they?' asked Ignatius.

Before the boy could reply Mrs Sculthorpe clapped her hands. 'Will you all look this way, please?' she said.

Most of us stopped talking.

'And that includes you, Michael Sidebottom.'

Everything went quiet.

'This morning we are going to write a poem. I want you all to think about the sea. Now, as you know, we have done quite a lot of work about the coast in preparation for our school trip to Whitby in a couple of weeks' time.'

'Miss!'

'Yes, what is it, Barry?'

'Miss, my dad nearly got drowned last year at Blackpool. He was swept out to sea on this twenty-foot wave.'

We all burst out laughing.

'Miss, it's true, he swam out to get this ball for a little girl, it had been carried out to sea by the wind, and this great big wave carried him off. It took him ages to swim back to shore and – '

'Miss!' shouted Valerie Harper. 'Miss, my sister was bitten by a jellyfish last year when she was in Filey.'

'I don't think jellyfish actually bite, Valerie,' said Ignatius. 'They sting but I don't think they –'

'Miss, they do,' insisted Valerie. 'There was a big red blotch on her leg where it bit her.'

The class again burst into laughter.

'Miss, when we went to see my Auntie Monica in Dublin last year,' said Kevin Murphy, 'we were coming through customs and they stopped my grandma and made her go in this room and take all her clothes off.'

Mrs Sculthorpe sighed and then turned to Jean-Paul, who was staring seriously out of the window.

'Do you live near the sea, Jean-Paul?' she asked pleasantly.

'Yes, I do,' he replied. 'But where I live eet is warm and there is not the shell.'

'He means the smell, miss,' I explained. 'Probably from the tannery on Common Lane.'

'Thank you, James,' said the teacher. 'I don't know how we managed to get on to the tannery on Common Lane. I started talking about the sea. Anyway, I've brought in a collection of shells this morning and in a minute I'm going to put some on each desk. I want you to look very carefully at the shells, notice what colour they are and the shape and feel, and then we are going to write a poem or a description – a sort of picture in words. Yes, what is it now, Kevin?'

'Miss, last year when we were on holiday at my Auntie Monica's in Dublin, we went to the sea and my cousin Attracta stood on a shell and her foot swelled up like a balloon and went all purple and yellow and she had to go into hospital where this doctor got a kind of knife thing and cut right into her.'

'Thank you, Kevin. I've already told you that we've heard quite enough of your Irish relations for one day. Now I want you all to write a colourful and interesting poem or short description about your shell. This one is flat and bumpy with tiny holes in it, and this one on Barry's desk is sharp and spiky and blue. There's quite a variety – clam, cockle, cowrie, mussel, whelk and winkle. We will no doubt add to our collection after our visit to Whitby. So, I want you all to look very closely at your shell and use your imaginations.'

Mrs Sculthorpe then went round the classroom giving out shells of all sizes and shapes and colours. Soon we had settled down to work and all you could hear was the scratching of pens. After ten minutes I had written about the shell in front of me and was very pleased with my effort:

I can see a white shell, clean and polished,
It curls and twists and shines like a pearl.
There are tiny grains of sand clinging to it
And it smells of the sea.

I looked at Jean-Paul's paper. It hadn't a thing written on it. He was still staring out of the window and looked as bored as my mum when our next-door neighbour tells her about all her medical problems. I looked over to where Mrs Sculthorpe was whispering loudly in Kevin Murphy's ear.

'You just did not listen, did you, Kevin? I asked for a poem or a short description about a shell, not a story about a killer clam that devours deep-sea divers and spits out their bones. Now start again and do as you were told.'

'Yes, miss.'

Then Mrs Sculthorpe headed in my direction. She peered over my shoulder. 'Oh yes, I like this, James. You describe your shell very well.' Then she caught sight of Jean-Paul with his empty sheet of paper. 'Didn't you understand what you had to do, Jean-Paul?' she asked.

'*Oui*, but I did not do it.'

'I beg your pardon?' The smile on Mrs Sculthorpe's face suddenly disappeared.

'This ees not the proper Engleesh. This is, how you say, my waste of time.'

Mrs Sculthorpe's face was now sort of screwed up, as if she were sucking a lemon. Her neck was all red and blotchy. The last time she had looked like that was when Barry Bannister had brought his ferret into the classroom and it had ended up in her shopping bag.

'Not the proper English? Whatever do you mean, Jean-Paul? Tell me, what is the proper English?' She said the last three words really slowly. Everyone was looking at the French boy.

'In France Madame Poisson learns us the proper Engleesh. Before I am coming to England I learn about the proberbs.'

'Really? The proverbs,' corrected Mrs Sculthorpe.

'My English teacher, Madame Poisson, she is very good at Engleesh. She tests us every week on the proberbs. A bird in the hand is worth two of them in the bushes; every cloud has the silver lining; people what are in glass houses should not be throwing the stones; it is like a pig in a china poke.'

Mrs Sculthorpe smiled. It was not a pleasant smile this time. 'Well, for your information, Jean-Paul, English people rarely use *proverbs* any more.'

'Madame Poisson says all Engleesh people use the proberbs,' he announced.

'Well, I'm afraid your Madame Poisson is wrong. The word is *proverbs*, by the way, and very few people use them these days.'

'Madame Poisson, she teaches me about zer verbs and zer nouns and zer sentences. This ees the proper English.'

Mrs Sculthorpe breathed out. We could see she was really mad.

'Well, Jean-Paul, dear,' she said quietly, 'it won't be too long now before you are back in the classroom of the excellent Madame Poisson, learning the proper English, but until then you are in my classroom and you must follow the very famous proverb which I am sure you are only too familiar with: "When in Rome you do as the Romans do." So get on with the description of your shell.'

Over the next couple of weeks Jean-Paul didn't find much to his liking. The headmaster was a *fool*, the school dinners were 'only for zer pigs', Mr Wilson, who took the boys for games, could not 'referee a game of tiddlywinks'. He refused to let the nit nurse look at his hair – 'French people do not have the creatures on the head' – or the school dentist examine his teeth. When the school photographer asked him to 'smile please' he replied, 'What is there to be smiling at?' He was a real pain in the neck. And he went on and on about Mrs Sculthorpe not teaching the proper English.

It was a bright and sunny day when Mr Griddle, the headmaster, came into our classroom. I don't like Mr Griddle. As far as I can tell he doesn't do much apart from water the plants in the entrance hall and shout at us in assembly. He also has his favourites – usually the kids whose parents live in the big houses and pass their eleven plus exam to go on to King Henry's, the grammar school up the hill. He sort of whines when he speaks, as if he's got a permanent cold and his nose is all bunged up.

'You will all look this way a moment,' he droned. 'And that includes you, Michael Sidebottom. Now, next Monday we will be having two very important visitors. The Mayor and Lady Mayoress, Councillor and Mrs Farrington, will be with us for part of the morning, looking around the school and joining us for assembly. I want everybody, and that includes you, Barry Bannister and Kevin Murphy, to be on his or her very, very best behaviour. I do not want the Mayor to return to his office with a poor impression of St Jude's. Being the top class in the school you will be reading out some of your work. Mrs Sculthorpe has spoken to me very highly of the stories and poems you have written.' Then he looked to where Jean-Paul was sitting, staring out of the window, with a bored expression on his face. 'Perhaps, Jean-Paul, you might like to read something you have written?' We all expected him to shake his head but to our surprise he agreed.

'*Oui*, I will read something special,' he said.

'Splendid, splendid,' said Mr Griddle, rubbing his hands.

On the Monday morning we all filed into the hall for the assembly. The Mayor and Mayoress in their golden chains sat in pride of place on the front row, next to a self-important-looking Mr Griddle.

Six of us had been picked to read out our poems. Ignatius's was by far the best. When he had finished, I saw the Mayor turn to whisper something to the headmaster. Mr Griddle nodded.

Then it was Jean-Paul's turn. He produced a piece of paper from his pocket, cleared his throat and proceeded to read in French in a loud voice. I think it was the first time I had seen him smile. At first there was a little twist at the corners of his mouth but then it spread into a wide grin.

'Thank you very much, children,' said the headmaster. 'That was very good. And a special thank you to our visitor, Jean-Paul. I don't speak French myself but I am sure that what you wrote was most interesting.'

'Hey,' I said to Jean-Paul when we got back to the classroom. 'You went on a bit. I thought you were never going to stop.'

'I didn't understand a word you were saying,' Barry Bannister told him.

'Neither did I,' said Kevin.

'What did you say?' I asked him.

Jean-Paul thought for a moment and then a smile spread across his face. 'I said the headmaster is a fool. I said the school dinners are like the food for pigs. I said England is cold and stinks and I said the teacher does not speak the proper Engleesh.'

'Crikey! You said all that?'

'*Oui*.'

'It's a good job Mr Griddle and the teachers and the Mayor didn't know what you were saying.' Then I started to chuckle.

We must have looked a comical pair when Mrs Sculthorpe walked in.

'My, my,' she said, 'you two look happy today.' Then she looked at Jean-Paul. 'Remember the old English proverb, won't you, Jean-Paul: "He who laughs last laughs longest."'

'Oh, *oui*,' he said, shrugging.

'And what are you laughing at, James Johnson?' asked Mrs Sculthorpe.

~

☆ 6 ☆

THE CAKE

I have to admit I do love my food. I love burgers: those thick, juicy circles of beef sandwiched between soft bread and smothered in lip-smacking ketchup. I love crispy battered fish and steaming chips, crunchy crisps, fat sizzling sausages and pizza topped with bright red tomatoes and delicious melted cheese. Of course, like most lads of my age, I love crispy cones with strawberry and vanilla ice cream dribbling down the sides, thick slabs of milk chocolate, boiled sweets and chewy toffee. But my favourite, my very favourite, is the coffee and walnut cake Mum makes on special occasions.

The very thought of a thick wedge of that pale brown sponge layered with creamy filling and topped with a crust of thick sweet icing and a ring of walnuts makes my mouth water uncontrollably.

One Saturday morning I wandered into the kitchen and there in pride of place on the table was a coffee and walnut cake. My eyes grew to the size of saucers. I gave a great heaving sigh and smiled. 'Coffee and walnut cake,' I mouthed.

'Don't you touch that, young man,' said Mum, catching sight of me drooling in front of the cake. 'It's not for you.' My heart sank right down into my trainers. 'Your Auntie Myra and Uncle Norman are coming round this afternoon for tea.' I was speechless and continued to gaze at the cake. 'If there's any left then you can have a slice.'

I soon found my tongue. 'Any left!' I spluttered. 'Not much chance of that with Auntie Myra and Uncle Norman. They eat like starving dinosaurs. There won't be so much as a crumb left.'

'If I have time,' Mum told me, seeing my obvious disappointment, 'I'll make another one next week.'

'I've heard that before,' I said.

'And any more out of you, young man,' said Mum, 'and there will be no cake for you next week.'

Later that morning, try as I might, I just could not take my mind off the cake. I lay on my bed, eyes closed, and the picture of the delicious confection floated into my mind: the soft sponge, creamy filling, thick crust of icing and crunchy walnuts.

'I'm off to the shops, Jimmy!' Mum shouted up the

stairs. 'Do you want anything?'

'A thick chunk of coffee and walnut cake, that's what,' I murmured to myself. 'No thanks!' I shouted back to Mum.

When the door banged shut I crept down the stairs. I just had to have a peek at the cake. It could do no harm, just to see it and savour it. I opened the pantry door charily and peered inside. There it was on the bottom shelf, sitting on a pale blue china plate with a cake knife next to it. I noticed that some of the icing on the top had

drizzled down the side. I picked it off and popped it in my mouth. Mmmm, delicious. A bit of the sponge had come away with the icing so I just had to eat that too. Now one side of the cake looked different from the other, so, to even things up, I cut a small sliver off. The sponge melted in my mouth. Then a walnut fell off. Crunch! Crunch! Scrumptious. The cake now looked as if it had been attacked by a ravenous mouse. It was ruined.

Now what was I going to do, I thought. I remembered that the Rumbling Tum Bakery on the high street in town sold cakes. There's nothing for it, I said to myself, I shall have to raid my money-box, cycle into town and buy a replacement. I just hoped that there would be a coffee and walnut cake left and that Mum would not notice the substitution. But what about the remains of the cake which now sat there all forlorn-looking on the blue china plate, I thought. Nothing for it – I shall have to eat it. So – I devoured the lot.

'Sorry, son,' said the baker at the Rumbling Tum Bakery, 'I've just sold the last coffee and walnut cake. They're very popular. You could try the corner shop on Church Street. They sometimes have cakes in the freezer but they're not as nice as mine.'

I cycled at a mad speed down to the corner shop

on Church Street. The cake I had eaten earlier began to churn in my stomach and by the time I had chained my bicycle up to a lamp-post I was feeling decidedly ill. Ignoring the sickly taste in my mouth and the grumbling pain in my stomach, I rushed into the shop. There was a big chest freezer by the wall and standing by it was Michael's mum. As I drew closer I saw she was holding … a coffee and walnut cake. She was just about to pop it into her wire basket.

'Hello, James,' she said. Mrs Sidebottom was a big round woman with bright blonde hair, lipstick the colour of blood, and eyes with so much black make-up on, she looked like a giant panda.

'Hello, Mrs Sidebottom,' I said.

'Doing a bit of shopping for your mother?' she asked. Before I could reply she said, 'Michael has his pianoforte tuition on Saturday mornings. He's getting really very good. The teacher says he has a musical ear. This afternoon his father is taking him to town to get him a new anorak and some walking boots for the trip to Whitby next week. Then it won't be long before you take your eleven plus examination for the grammar school. Michael's father is going to have him measured up for the blazer in town this afternoon.'

Suppose he doesn't pass the eleven plus, I thought to myself, but I didn't say anything.

'He's having private tuition, you know,' Mrs Sidebottom told me, 'just to be on the safe side. Miss Peacock is tutoring him in mathematics and English. All her pupils get through. And how are you getting on at school, James?' she asked. 'Would you like to go to the grammar school with Michael?'

'I don't really know,' I told her. 'I've not thought about it much.' I edged past her to get to the freezer. I peered inside. There was no sign of a coffee and walnut cake. There were mince tarts, strawberry flans, Victoria sponges, apple pies and Swiss rolls but no coffee and walnut cake. Mrs Sidebottom had got the last one.

'I suppose Michael told you about my food poisoning,' I whispered, so the shopkeeper who was busy serving a queue of customers couldn't hear.

'No, he hasn't,' she said. 'I thought the school dinners were very good at St Jude's.'

'No, not at the school. Mum bought a cake from here last week and I was sick all night. Couldn't keep a thing down.'

'Oh dear,' she said.

'Evidently some nuts were off. Walnuts actually. Like

the nuts in your cake, or it could have been the cream filling. Anyway, I was really ill.'

Mrs Sidebottom examined the packet. It was a fancy box with a picture of a smiling round-faced woman on the front. 'Mrs Baxter's Coffee and Walnut Cake' it said on the packet. 'Just like the cakes your mother used to make.'

'This is Michael's favourite cake,' she said. 'However, in light of what you've just said I don't think I'll risk it.' She placed the cake back in the freezer.

'Very wise,' I said nodding.

I waited until she had paid for the groceries in her basket and left the shop. My heart leapt for joy. It looked from the picture on the packet exactly like the one Mum had baked earlier that day. I was saved.

My elation evaporated at the counter. I passed over all the change from my money-box.

'Take it out of that,' I said.

The miserable-looking young woman behind the counter pulled a sour face when she saw the pile of silver and copper. She counted it out behind the counter. 'I need another five pence.'

'What?' I exclaimed.

'Another five pence,' repeated the woman sullenly.

'But that's all the money I've got,' I said sadly.

'Well, you can't have it then, can you?' she said, examining a broken nail.

'I haven't got another five pence.'

'Tough,' she said.

'The cake's for my poor disabled granny's birthday,' I pleaded. 'She's sick in hospital.'

'Can't help that,' said the woman unsympathetically. 'You'll have to put it back if you can't pay for it.'

'Here, love,' said an elderly woman who was behind me in the queue. She thrust five pence into my hand. 'It's nice to see young people caring for the old.' She gave the assistant behind the counter a savage look. 'You've got your measly five pence now,' she said.

'Thanks,' I said.

It was quite a job, but I managed to defrost the cake (with the help of Mum's hairdrier) and place it on the blue plate in the pantry. I smiled. It looked pretty much like the one Mum had baked.

Later that afternoon, when Auntie Myra and Uncle Norman arrived, Mum asked me to bring the cake through to the front room. I did so with a smug expression on my face.

'What a lovely cake,' said Auntie Myra. 'It looks

delicious, as light as a feather. You always make lovely cakes, Brenda. It's such a pity I can't have any.'

'Can't have any?' I spluttered.

'No,' said Auntie Myra. 'I'm on a diet. Too many calories in that cake, I'm afraid.'

'What about you, Uncle Norman?' asked Mum. 'I'm sure you'd like a piece.'

'Thank you, no, Brenda,' he said. 'I'd love a slice but I've developed this nut allergy. I can't eat walnuts. They bring me out in a rash.'

'Well,' said Mum, smiling at me, 'it looks as if you're in luck, young man.'

My stomach began doing somersaults and I felt the colour drain from my face. The very thought of another piece of coffee and walnut cake made me feel sick. 'Get the knife, will you, love,' said Mum, with a knowing smile on her face, 'and I'll cut you a nice fat slice.'

~

☆ 7 ☆

THE SCHOOL TRIP

'It seems pretty straightforward to me, Mrs Sculthorpe,' said the headmaster in that high whining tone of voice. 'If he hasn't brought the money, then he can't go. It's as simple as that.'

'That seems very unfair to me,' said my teacher. 'He will be the only child in my class who isn't going.'

I was outside Mr Griddle's door listening in to the conversation. It was morning break and I had been sent there by the caretaker to tell the headmaster that the pipes in the boys' toilets were leaking again, but I thought I would wait to knock at the door, which stood ajar, and listen in. The conversation sounded very interesting, and I soon learnt who the subject of their discussion was. It was Ignatius Plunket.

'Mrs Sculthorpe,' said the headmaster, 'you really cannot expect the school to come up with the money for the trip. I mean, if we were to pay for one pupil then the floodgates would open and all the parents would be expecting the school trips to be free of charge.'

'I really don't think that is the case, Mr Griddle,' said Mrs Sculthorpe. I could tell she was angry by her tone of voice. 'You know the circumstances in the Plunket household. This is a special case.'

The headmaster gave a harrumph. 'I know the boy's circumstances only too well,' he said. 'He comes from a lazy and feckless family. His parents haven't done a day's work in their lives from what I can gather, they never attend school functions and they send him to school as if he's been dragged through a hedge backwards.'

'That is really not the boy's fault,' said Mrs Sculthorpe.

'His parents spend most of the time in the betting office or in the public house,' continued the headmaster. 'It's not as if they can't pay.'

'That is my point, Mr Griddle,' persisted Mrs Sculthorpe. 'They spend their money on other things and not on school trips for their children. It's not the poor boy's fault he can't find the money for the trip.'

'That may well be,' said Mr Griddle pompously, 'but I am not making any exception so there is really nothing further to discuss. The school is not subsidizing the trip and that is the end of the matter.'

'I see,' said Mrs Sculthorpe angrily. 'In that case I shall pay for the trip myself.'

'I really don't think that is a very good idea,' said the headmaster.

'It's my money, Mr Griddle, and how I choose to spend it is up to me. Good morning.'

I stood away from the door quickly and pretended to be examining the picture of a sailing ship on the wall.

'What are you doing here, James Johnson?' demanded Mrs Sculthorpe sharply.

'Miss,' I told her, looking all innocent, 'I've been sent by the caretaker to tell Mr Griddle that the pipes are leaking in the boys' toilets.'

'I hope you have not been eavesdropping?'

'Oh no, miss,' I lied. 'I was looking at this picture.'

She didn't look convinced, but clomped angrily away down the corridor.

I knew already that Ignatius was not going on the trip. On the way to school that Friday morning Micky Sidebottom had asked Ignatius if he had remembered to bring in the money for the school trip to Whitby the following day.

'Oh, I won't be going to Whitby,' Ignatius told us nonchalantly. He didn't appear all that bothered.

'Not going!' I exclaimed. 'Don't you want to go?'

'Oh yes,' he replied calmly. 'I would very much enjoy a trip to the seaside, it's just that things are a little tight financially at home at the moment.'

I always smiled when he used these fancy words and phrases. He sounded like an old man.

'You mean your parents won't cough up the cash,' said Micky bluntly.

'That's about right,' said Ignatius, giving a weak smile.

'It's only a few quid,' Micky informed him, as if he was telling Iggy something he didn't know. 'It won't break the bank.'

'Perhaps not,' said Ignatius, 'but my father and mother don't think I should go.'

'You'll have to stay here all day moping around with nothing to do while we are on the beach at Whitby,' said Micky.

'You don't need to rub it in,' I told him.

'Oh, I won't be moping around,' Ignatius said breezily. 'There are lots of things I can do. There's the library for a start and the museum and –'

'I could lend you the money, Iggy,' I interrupted.

'That's very kind of you, James, but you know what they say?'

'No,' I said, 'I don't know what they say.' I looked at him expecting an answer but he just stared ahead of him. 'What do they say?'

'Neither a borrower nor a lender be,' said Ignatius. 'Shakespeare, you know.'

'I don't know about Shakespeare,' I said, 'but it's really rotten that you can't come.'

'Never mind,' he said cheerfully. 'I've got a book out of the public library about the north-east coast and shall read up on Whitby while you are exploring it. I shall be there in spirit if not in body.'

'You do say some daft things,' said Micky. 'Half the time I don't know what you are on about.'

When I overheard Mrs Sculthorpe say to Mr Griddle later that morning that she would be paying for Ignatius to go on the trip, I was really pleased, but I kept it to myself.

On the way home on the Friday afternoon Ignatius volunteered the information before I raised it with him.

'I'll be going on the school trip to Whitby after all,' he informed Micky and me. 'Mrs Sculthorpe has told me there is a spare seat on the bus.'

'And you don't have to pay?' exclaimed Micky.

'Apparently not.'

'That's not fair. I mean we've all had to pay. How come you're getting a free trip?'

'Why don't you shut up?' I said. 'Your parents can afford the trip ten times over, so what are you moaning about? And if you don't stop whinging and being horrible, then you can find somebody else to go about with in Whitby.'

Micky looked deflated. 'I was only saying,' he said feebly.

'Well, don't!' I snapped.

The following morning I was up early. I was too excited to sleep in – something I liked to do on a Saturday morning. The coach was to set off outside the school gates at eight o'clock prompt, but at seven I was out of bed, washed, dressed and ready to go. Mum had laid out all my clothes the night before and when I got downstairs she was busy making me sandwiches in the kitchen. The table was set for breakfast.

'I've done you some egg and tomato,' she said when she caught sight of me walking into the kitchen. 'And there's a piece of cake and some crisps and a bottle of pop.'

'Thanks, Mum.'

'Your dad's gone to work but before he went he cleaned your boots and he's left you a bit of extra pocket money on the table. He told me to tell you to be careful. Beaches can be dangerous.'

'I will,' I said, thinking how lucky I was to have parents like mine.

Micky arrived at half past seven. He was kitted out like some Antarctic explorer in a dark green anorak with an imitation-fur-lined hood. The coat was full of pockets and pouches, zips and flaps. On his back was a large red rucksack and around his neck a pair of huge binoculars.

'Dad got me these new boots,' he told me, pointing to his feet. 'The man at the shop said they're proper walking boots, specially padded for comfort, lightweight, waterproof and heat resistant. I've also got a scarf, thermal gloves, woolly hat and heavy duty socks.'

I shook my head. 'We're only going to Whitby,' I told him, 'not up Everest.'

'Well, Mrs Sculthorpe told us to get well wrapped up,' he said. 'It's going to be cold and wet.'

'I don't know why your teacher's taking you to the seaside in this weather,' Mum told us.

'It's a field trip, Mrs Johnson,' explained Micky. 'We're going to study the coastal features as part of our geography work at school. Mrs Sculthorpe calls it "first hand experience".'

'Well, I still think it would have been better going in the summer when it's warmer,' said Mum.

We met Ignatius at the end of the road, casually walking along with a plastic bag in one hand and a book in the other. He was wearing bright blue Wellington boots with flowery patterns round the top, a greasy brown coat with the sleeves turned up and the same grey baggy trousers with the shiny bottom which he wore for school. A long multicoloured woollen scarf was wrapped around his neck like some huge snake, and on his head was a flat cap, the kind that old men wear.

We caught up with him. 'What have you got on your feet?' asked Micky, staring at the bright blue Wellingtons. 'They're the sort girls wear.' I eyed Micky with an expression which told him to keep his mouth shut.

'They're my mother's,' said Ignatius, unconcerned by the comment. 'My boots are too small, so I'm borrowing hers. I have to admit that they are rather dazzling but they're quite comfortable and won't let in the water, which is the main thing, isn't it?'

'Shall I put your things in my rucksack?' I asked him.

'That's all right, James,' said Ignatius. 'There are only my sandwiches and a bottle of water. Thanks anyway.'

The coach, an old green vehicle which had seen better days, arrived fifteen minutes late. At ten minutes past eight o'clock, still with no sign of the coach, Mrs Sculthorpe, dressed in a bright red duffel coat and a matching scarf and bobble hat, went into school to phone the firm to see where it had got to. When she disappeared through the school entrance the coach chugged up puthering out smoke from the exhaust.

'Not very environmentally friendly,' observed Ignatius, to no one in particular.

The driver, a grumpy-looking little man with a shiny bald head and a face as brown and wrinkled as an overripe apple, ordered us to line up quietly and listen.

'Now, you kids,' he growled, 'I don't want anyone messing about on my bus. There will be no toilet stop, so make sure you've all been before you get on. There's a plastic bucket at the front for anyone who feels sick, so use it. I don't want anyone vomiting on my seats. I want no litter on the floor, no shouting or running about, no singing, no making faces through the windows at the motorists and no touching the emergency door at the back.'

'Unless, of course, there's an emergency,' said Ignatius innocently.

'Eh?'

'If there is an emergency,' continued Ignatius, unaware of the sniggers from those around him, 'we will then need to make use of the emergency door.'

'Are you being cheeky?' asked the driver, getting red in the face.

'No, just pointing it out,' said Ignatius.

'Well, don't!' snapped the driver. 'And there's no talking to the driver as well.'

Mrs Sculthorpe appeared, not looking all that pleased.

'I was just telling these kids,' said the grouchy driver, 'that I want no messing about on my bus.'

'There is really no need,' Mrs Sculthorpe told him brusquely. 'My class is very well behaved.'

'Aye, and I've heard that one before,' grumbled the driver.

'Shall we be on our way then?' asked the teacher. 'We are late.'

'I was delayed. You want to see the state of the roads –' began the driver.

Mrs Sculthorpe held up a hand as if stopping traffic. 'Then we had better waste no more time, had we?' she told him.

'Good morning, miss,' said Ignatius when she counted us as we boarded the coach.

'Good morning, Ignatius,' she replied, glancing down at his boots and giving a little smile. 'Are you looking forward to the trip?'

'Oh yes, miss,' he said. 'I've never been to the seaside.'

'Never?' she exclaimed.

'No,' he replied. 'It will be very interesting.'

'I am sure it will,' she said.

We arrived at Whitby just after ten. Mrs Sculthorpe instructed the driver to collect us at one o'clock, when we would be going up the coast to Robin Hood's Bay for the afternoon to explore the beaches and do our coastal study. He grunted and lit a cigarette. 'And please don't be late,' she said.

We spent the morning looking around Whitby, climbing up the 199 steps to the abbey, visiting the museum and Captain Cook's house and having a guided tour around a great masted sailing ship called *The Grand Turk*, which was moored at the quay. We had our sandwiches sitting on the wall, listening to the seagulls circling in the air and the loud music in the amusement arcades along the front.

'This is amazing,' said Ignatius looking around him. 'Amazing.'

At Robin Hood's Bay that afternoon we headed for the beach down a steep hill, Mrs Sculthorpe in front, giving a running commentary about what we could see. Then we made our way through a series of narrow cobbled walkways between small stone cottages with whitewashed walls and roofs of orange tiles and grey slates. The houses seemed to cling to the cliff side. Barry and Kevin had attached themselves to us and I was getting sick and tired of their constant moaning.

'In the olden days,' Ignatius told us, like a guide, 'the smugglers unloaded all their contraband and carried it to the top of village through a maze of secret tunnels underneath the cottages to evade the customs men. I've read in my book –'

'That's really interesting,' interrupted Kevin, looking bored. 'But will you shut up. You sound like a teacher going on and on.'

'I'm starving,' moaned Barry. 'I hope there are some shops at the bottom. And just think of the walk back up to the top. It'll be like climbing a mountain.'

'I'm cold,' complained Micky. 'And I'm getting wet.'

'What about your specially padded walking boots, thermal gloves and heavy duty socks?' I said. 'Some good they are.'

'I'm still cold,' he moaned.

On the beach Mrs Sculthorpe gathered us around her.

'Now everybody look this way,' she said, 'and that does include you, Barry Bannister and Kevin Murphy. Put that piece of driftwood down and listen. It's cold, wet and windy this afternoon and as you can see we have the beach to ourselves.'

'I'm not surprised,' muttered Micky. 'I'm like a block of ice.'

'We have an hour here to explore the beach,' continued the teacher, 'looking for interesting pebbles, fossils and unusual shells. I want you to be especially careful.' She stopped. 'What do I want you to be, Barry Bannister?' she asked.

'Pardon, miss?'

'In one ear and out the other!' exclaimed the teacher. 'I said, I want you to be especially careful. Beaches can be dangerous places. No running about on the slippery rocks, no going in the sea or climbing up the cliffs. Stay on the sand and behave yourselves and meet me back here at three o'clock. Is that understood?'

'Yes, miss,' chorused the class.

'I'm not looking for stupid fossils and shells,' Barry told us as we walked off along the sands. 'I'm off to explore the caves. If there were smugglers here there might be hidden booty.'

'I don't think that's very likely,' said Ignatius. 'It would have been discovered years ago.'

'Ooooh, I don't think that's very likely,' mimicked Barry. 'Come on, Kev, I'll race you to the rocks.'

'You heard what Mrs Sculthorpe said,' I told him.

'You're getting to sound like Plunket,' Barry shouted back. 'Anyway, she didn't say anything about caves, did she?'

'All the same –' began Ignatius.

'Can I come, Barry?' asked Micky. 'I don't want to look for fossils and shells either.'

'Are you coming, JJ?' asked Kevin.

'No, I'm stopping with Iggy,' I told him.

The three of them ran off shouting and laughing and kicking sand in every direction and left Ignatius and me looking for shells and fossils.

Ten minutes later Barry came running up to us, red in the face and out of breath.

'Can you come quick!' he yelled.

'What is it?' I asked.

'It's an emergency.' He began to tug at my sleeve. 'Come on, hurry up!'

'What's wrong?'

'It's Micky,' he told me, panting. 'He's stuck.'

'Stuck?' I repeated.

'In the mud.'

'In the mud?'

'Stop repeating me,' he screamed. 'Just come and help, will you? He's got himself stuck in the mud and he can't get out. He's in a real state.'

I started to laugh but Barry yelled in my face. 'It's not funny, Johnson, he's sinking.'

So Ignatius and I followed Barry until we came to the cliff bottom. The cliffs were steep and rocky but a great curtain of mud had slipped down and covered part of the beach. There up to his knees in a big mound of chocolate-coloured mud was Micky, wailing and tugging. 'Help me!' he cried. 'I'm stuck and I can't get out.'

Ignatius immediately took charge. 'Michael,' he said, 'you have to stay calm.'

'Oh great,' said Barry. 'He'll be up to his neck in mud in a minute and you say stay calm.'

'Michael,' said Ignatius, ignoring the comment, 'you have to remain calm and stop struggling. The more you move about, the more you'll sink.'

'Get Mrs Sculthorpe,' he moaned.

'We have to act quickly,' Ignatius told him. 'By the

time Mrs Sculthorpe arrives you'll be –' He stopped before completing the sentence.

Micky howled.

'How did he get stuck in the mud?' I asked Kevin, who had remained quiet and open-mouthed throughout.

'He climbed up the cliff side and then jumped off. He thought it was a big brown rock below him but it turned out to be this massive mound of mud with a sort of hard crust on the top. When he landed he went straight through it.'

'Stop talking and get me out!' cried Micky.

'Look, Michael,' said Ignatius, 'you must try not to get all upset, and don't struggle. You'll only make matters worse. We will get you out.'

'How?' asked Barry. 'Don't think I'm climbing up on to that mud. I'll sink too.'

'I saw a piece of pipe down the beach,' said Kevin. 'Micky could use it as a breathing tube when the mud goes over his head.'

'Ohhhhhhh,' whimpered Micky.

'I don't think you're being very helpful,' said Ignatius. He removed his long multicoloured scarf. 'Give me your scarf, Kevin.'

'What?'

'Your scarf. Give it to me.'

'Why?'

'Just give it to me, and yours, James, and yours, Barry. I intend to tie them all together to create a makeshift rope and we will pull him out.'

'And how will we do that?' asked Barry.

'I'll show you,' said Ignatius calmly.

He knotted the several scarves together, made a loop at one end like a lasso and climbed up the cliff side, positioning himself directly above Micky. He lowered the scarves.

'Put the loop over your head,' he told Micky, 'and then under your arms.' He turned to us on the beach. 'I do need some help. You three come up here and give me a hand.' Slowly but surely we heaved and Micky was pulled from the mud. He scrambled on to the cliff side and then climbed into the sand, where he collapsed and began sobbing. 'I could have died! I could have died!' he howled.

'That was amazing,' I told Ignatius.

'I read this story about a famous sleuth,' he told me.

'A what?'

'A detective. Sherlock Holmes had fallen into a deep slimy bog and was sinking, and Dr Watson, his companion, managed to get him out by remaining calm and collected and deciding on a clear plan of action. The important thing is not to panic.'

'He could have gone under,' said Barry in a gruesome voice. 'He could have sunk without trace. Just think, choking and drowning in mud.'

'Will you shut up, Barry,' I said.

Micky soon calmed down and was unusually quiet on the way back.

'You had better wash your boots in the sea, Michael,' said Ignatius. 'I have a feeling that that grumpy bus driver won't let you on his coach in that state. And I think we could rinse through our scarves as well.'

We all did as he suggested.

'My goodness,' said Mrs Sculthorpe when she caught sight of this group of mud-caked boys tramping along the sand towards her, holding their wet scarves 'You look as if you've been swimming in mud, you boys. Just look at the state of you all.'

'Michael slipped,' explained Ignatius. 'We went to help him.'

'Well, I hope you all have something to write about when we get back to school.'

Ignatius looked at me, smiled and winked. 'Oh yes, Mrs Sculthorpe,' he said.

☆ 8 ☆

THE EXAM

The long-awaited day finally arrived. I sat opposite Mum at the breakfast table fingering a piece of toast, with my stomach doing kangaroo jumps.

'Come on, love,' said Mum, 'eat your breakfast. You don't want to go to school on an empty stomach, particularly today.'

'I'm not hungry,' I told her sighing miserably.

'You've got to have something. You don't want to go and faint in the middle of it all.'

'I won't,' I said.

It was the day of the dreaded eleven plus examination. In the 1950s every pupil in their last year at primary school across the whole of the country sat the eleven plus, sitting down with a big thick test paper in front of them, trying to answer the questions on English and arithmetic and general knowledge.

At school we had been building up to this day for

a good few weeks now, practising our spellings, being tested every morning in mental arithmetic, writing stories in half an hour, doing boring comprehension tests about the life cycle of the butterfly or dairy farming in the Yorkshire Dales or how they constructed the Panama Canal. Now the day of reckoning had finally arrived and I felt awful. My head throbbed, my chest hurt and my stomach jumped up and down.

The dreaded eleven plus examination decided which pupils in the town would go to King Henry's College, the grammar school at the top of the hill, and which would end up at Sunny Grove Secondary Modern at the bottom. Mum had set her heart on me going to the grammar. She didn't go on and on about it like Michael's mum, who seemed to think about nothing else, but I knew she was really keen for me to get through the eleven plus so that I 'would get a decent job with good prospects'. As an eleven-year-old, interested only in football, comics and model aeroplanes, a decent job with good prospects was the last thing on my mind.

For the last few weeks Mum had gone through my spellings every night, given me maths problems to solve, set me timed essays and even bought me some practice papers from the bookshop in town.

Every Friday, when she was paid, she had taken some money out of her wage packet and put it into a tin which she kept on the top of the kitchen cupboard. I knew that this was for my school uniform if I should pass my eleven plus. The letter she'd received from the school a few weeks previously had explained that those who were successful in getting a place at the grammar school – and very few were fortunate enough to do so, it added – would have to be equipped with a white shirt, school tie, black blazer, grey flannel trousers, grey socks and black shoes, all to be bought from Seymour and Son, High Class Family Outfitters, on the high street. They would also need a full football/rugby strip in the school colours and boots and a PE kit and regulation plimsolls. Each article of clothing had to have a name label on. These could be ordered from Seymour and Son. Then there would be a satchel, fountain pen, pocket school dictionary and the school hymnbook to buy. It added up to a lot of money, so Mum had started saving at the beginning of the year.

'Come along now,' said Mum. 'I think it's about time you were going.'

I sat frozen to my seat. What if I couldn't answer one

single question? What if I knew nothing about what was on the paper? Mum reached over the table and put her hand on mine. 'Just do your best, love, that's all you can do. If you pass, then all very well and good. If you don't, well, it's not the end of the world, is it?'

I met Micky on the way to school. He looked as nervous as a lamb in a cage full of lions.

'My mum's in a real state today,' he told me. 'It's as if *she* was sitting the flipping exam. She was up at five o'clock this morning and she never shut up at breakfast. My dad went to work early. He told her she was getting neurotic and he couldn't stand it any longer.'

We soon caught up with Ignatius Plunket, dawdling along as usual with his head in a book. It seemed to him like any other day. He didn't seem to have a worry in the world.

'It's all right for you, Iggy,' said Micky gloomily, pulling up alongside of him.

'What is?' asked Ignatius, looking up and squinting in Michael's direction.

'You'll sail through the eleven plus,' said Micky, looking gloomier than ever. 'You could do it standing on your head, blindfolded with your hands tied behind your back.'

'I don't know about that,' replied Ignatius, smiling.

'Course you will, Iggy,' I said. 'It's just up your street, all those general knowledge questions and problem solving and story writing.'

'I've been sick three times this morning,' Micky confided in us. 'All over the bedroom, the bathroom floor and down the stairs. Mum would have gone mad normally because we've just had a new carpet fitted, but this morning she told me to leave it and she'd clean it up. It would take her mind off things.'

'I hope there's not too much arithmetic,' I said, not really listening to his ramblings.

'I really don't think I can go through with it,' said Micky suddenly, stopping in his tracks. 'I didn't sleep a wink last night. What happens if you're ill and can't sit the paper?'

'You do it later,' Ignatius told him, 'up at the grammar school, and, of course, they give you a different paper.'

'Best get it over with today,' I said.

'Just do your best,' said Ignatius cheerfully. 'You can't do any more than that. You'll be fine, Michael, you really will.'

'That's all very well, Iggy,' said our despondent companion, 'but my mum has set her sights on me getting through. My cousin Oliver, who lives in Harrogate, passed his eleven plus last year and we've never heard the last of it from my Auntie Doreen. I think my mum would commit suicide if I failed. I tell you the pressure is getting me down. It's making me sick as a parrot. I've already tried on a blazer at Seymour's. Then, of course, my mum and dad have shelled out a lot of money for me to have private tuition as well.'

'I know,' I said, 'your mum told me.'

'I've been going to Miss Peacock on Ramsden Road every Saturday morning for the last few weeks. She's a retired teacher and has been helping me with my maths and English. She's a flipping slave driver is Miss 'Know-it-all' Peacock. She's given me lists of words and phrases to learn so that I can use them when I write my essay and she goes through my work with a great big red pen. It looks as if she's had a nosebleed all over the paper, there's so much red on the page. And I'm sick to death of flipping practice papers.'

'Well, it will all be over in a couple of hours,' said Ignatius calmly. 'Just try and take it in your stride.'

'As I said, it's all right for you, Iggy,' said Michael. 'You'll sail through the paper.'

The atmosphere at school was very different that morning. Instead of screaming children running round the playground, boys booting footballs and girls skipping, there were knots of glum-looking pupils chattering quietly by the school wall.

When the whistle blew, we all filed into school quietly and down the corridor to the hall where we were to sit the exam. We must have looked like a lot of condemned prisoners going to our execution. All of us, that is, except Ignatius, who still ambled along with his nose in a book. As we waited outside the school hall, I caught sight of Mrs Sculthorpe rushing around like a jam-crazed wasp, putting pencils, rubbers, rulers and sheets of paper on each desk. She looked more nervous than anyone.

When we were seated, Mr Griddle, the headmaster, came in carrying a large brown envelope which he placed on the desk at the very front.

'Now, I want you all to listen very, very carefully,' he whined. 'Ignatius, would you put your book away now, please, and look this way. In ten minutes you will have in front of you your eleven plus paper and you will have one hour and a half to complete it. The first thing to do is print your name clearly at the top of the paper. Then you will work your way through the questions, making sure you have not missed a page. If you finish before the hour and a half is up, then you should go through the paper carefully and check over what you have written. Answer all the questions. If you don't think you can answer a question then have a guess. Writing something is better than writing nothing. Now is there anything anyone wishes to ask?'

Micky's hand shot up. 'May I go to the toilet please, sir?' he asked.

The headmaster sighed, glanced at his wrist watch and said, 'Very well, but be quick about it.' Michael scurried off. 'If anyone else wishes to visit the lavatory, do it now, because you will not be allowed out of the hall during the examination.'

The paper wasn't half as bad as I thought it would be. The essay – to write about a favourite seaside place – was one we had written for Mrs Sculthorpe a few weeks back, so that was a real stroke of luck. I wrote three pages on the trip to Whitby. The arithmetic presented no real problems and I answered every question. The comprehension, where we had to answer twenty questions on a set passage about the history of railways, was hard and boring but I managed to finish just before Mr Griddle told us to put down our pens.

'I'm so glad that's over,' said Michael on the way home. 'It's like a big flipping hundred-ton weight being lifted from off my shoulders. It's just the wait now. My mum will be like a cat on a hot tin roof for the next three weeks until the results come out.'

'It wasn't too bad a paper,' I said. 'I thought it would be a lot harder. What did you think, Iggy?' Ignatius was walking along with us, looking neither pleased with himself nor downcast.

'Not too bad,' he repeated.

'I bet you got full marks,' said Micky. 'That essay you wrote for Mrs Sculthorpe a few weeks ago about the trip to Whitby, she read it out it was so good. Fancy that question about a visit to a seaside place coming up. I suppose the maths was a doddle for you as well. And everyone knows how interested you are in railways, Iggy.'

Ignatius didn't say anything.

I completely forgot about the eleven plus until one Saturday morning three weeks later. Mum got me up early. 'Come on, sleepy-head, let's have you downstairs. It's the day the eleven plus results come out.'

I shot out of bed like a rabbit with the runs and rushed downstairs. 'Has the postman been?' I asked, jumping up and down.

'Not yet,' said Mum. I could tell she was trying to keep calm.

The wait seemed endless, but just before nine o'clock a brown envelope dropped through the letterbox.

We both stared at it lying on the carpet in the hall, and then Mum said, 'Do you want to open it?'

'No, you,' I said. 'I can't.'

Mum picked up the envelope and, taking a knife from the kitchen table, slit open the flap. I could see her hand was trembling. She breathed out noisily, took out a white piece of paper and read it slowly.

'Well?' I said. My heart was in my mouth.

'You've passed,' she said really quietly. 'You passed. You got through to the grammar school.'

I yelped for joy and ran round and round the kitchen screaming 'I've passed! I've passed!' at the top of my voice. I couldn't believe it. I snatched the letter from Mum and read it to make sure they hadn't made a mistake, but it was there in black and white. I was to start at King Henry's College on the 5th of September.

Later that morning Micky called round. He was like a cat which had discovered a bucket full of cream. His smile stretched right across his face. He too had passed.

'My mum's gone mad, telling all the neighbours, phoning everybody she knows. She was on the phone to my Auntie Doreen for ages. Dad's gone to play golf. He said she's getting worse. We're going into town this afternoon to get the uniform and a bike. Dad said I could have a new bike if I passed.'

'I'm really pleased you've got through,' I said. 'That

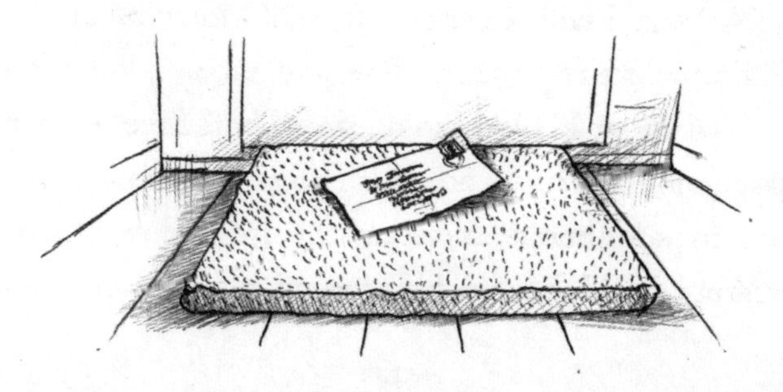

means there'll be at least two people I know going up to the grammar. Shall we go and see Iggy? I'd like to see his face when we tell him we'll be going to the grammar as well as him.'

'The thing is,' said Micky, looking at his feet, 'my mum said it might be best if I didn't hang about with Iggy when I'm up at the grammar school. She said he's ... well ... you know what he's like.'

'What do you mean, I know what he's like?' I asked. 'He's just like you and me and he's our pal, isn't he?'

'Mum thinks, well, she thinks he'll sort of drag me down.'

'Drag you down!' I repeated. 'Rather than drag you out, like he did when you were stuck in the mud?'

'She said it's all right me staying friends with you, though.'

'Oh, thanks very much,' I told him sarcastically. 'I'm glad your mum approves of me.'

'Anyway, I had better get off,' said Micky. 'I have to go into town.'

'You know, Micky,' I told him. 'I don't think I want to stay friends with you.'

I found Ignatius painting the front door. He was wearing a really grubby blue overall two sizes too big for him. He had black paint in his hair and on the tip of his long nose. 'I thought I would give the front door a lick of paint,' he told me. 'It's long overdue. My father would have done it, but he's allergic to paint.'

'We both got through to the grammar, Iggy,' I said. I wasn't as excited now after what Micky had said. 'Both Micky and me.'

'Congratulations,' he replied, continuing to paint the door.

'That means there'll be the three of us going up to King Henry's.'

Ignatius stopped painting. 'I won't be going to the grammar school, James,' said Ignatius.

'What!' I exclaimed. 'What do you mean you'll not be going?'

'I didn't pass,' he said simply.

'Didn't pass!' I gasped. 'You must have passed. You're the best in the class.'

'I didn't, I'm afraid,' said Ignatius. 'I got the letter this morning. I'm going to the secondary modern school.'

'You can't be,' I said. 'There must be some mistake.'

'It's down in black and white,' he said, starting to paint the door again.

I couldn't believe it. I just couldn't believe it. When I

told Mum I didn't expect the reply I got. She shook her head and said, 'Well, perhaps it's for the best.'

'What do you mean for the best?' I asked.

'Well, look, Jimmy, you have to admit Ignatius is a bit odd, isn't he, and just look at his home life. I mean, can you imagine his parents at parents' evening or at speech day or at the school play at King Henry's?'

'It's not his parents who are going,' I said. 'It's Ignatius and he deserves to go. He's brighter than any of us.'

'He would have had a real job fitting in at the grammar school,' said Mum.

'No, he wouldn't,' I said. 'He's really clever.'

'That's not what I mean,' said Mum. 'He might be the cleverest lad in the school but he won't fit in. He'll stand out like a sore thumb. You'll be mixing with a different class of people up at the grammar school. Dr Owen's lads go there and your headmaster's son. They're a different class of people to Ignatius and his family.'

'Perhaps I won't fit in, then,' I said, 'with all these snooty people.'

'Of course you will and you'll make me very proud of you.'

'But Ignatius's really clever, Mum,' I said. 'He deserves to go more than any of us.'

'We don't always get what we deserve, love,' Mum told me.

*

On Monday morning the pupils who had passed their eleven plus were summoned to Mr Griddle's room. I felt really special. There were twenty-five pupils in Mrs Sculthorpe's class and only Michael and me were going to the grammar school. Caroline Johnson, Pauline Wilmot and Valerie Harper were going to the girls' high school.

The headmaster stood behind his desk and shook hands with each of us in turn. 'You've done very well,' he said, 'and I am sure you will do credit to yourselves and to this school. It is a wonderful opportunity to have a grammar or a high school education. It leads to great things, so make the most of your time there. The work will be hard and there will be lots of it, but I am sure you will all rise to the challenge.'

'Thank you, sir,' we all said.

'Now,' Mr Griddle continued, 'I don't want any of you to go bragging about this in the school yard. Those children who did not get through will understandably be very disappointed. I don't want you showing off. Is that clear?'

'Yes, sir,' we all said.

'All right, you may return to your class.'

I called in at the boys' toilets on the way back to the classroom. I sat there in one of the cubicles thinking things over. I really didn't know whether I wanted to go to the grammar school after all. There would only be me and Michael there and I didn't know whether I wanted to be his friend any more. Then there was Mum, who had such high expectations – 'You'll make me very proud of you' – and Mr Griddle – 'The work will be hard and there will be lots of it.' Suppose I didn't fit in. I hadn't got much in common with Dr Owen's sons or Mr Griddle's. They didn't live in a terraced house with their mums working in a corner shop and their fathers at the steelworks. The more I thought about it, the more I didn't want to go.

I made my way back to the classroom feeling really down in the dumps and was just about to turn the corner in the corridor when I heard familiar voices. It was Mrs Sculthorpe and Ignatius.

'Whatever happened, Ignatius?' she was asking.

'I don't know, miss,' he replied.

'Well, I just can't understand it at all. The paper wasn't that hard, certainly not for somebody of your ability.'

'It's just one of those things,' Ignatius said.

'I think they must have got the papers mixed up,' said the teacher.

'It's very unlikely, miss, that there will be another boy with the name of Ignatius Plunket,' he replied.

'Well, something's gone drastically wrong,' said Mrs Sculthorpe. 'There must have been some dreadful mistake. It's beyond belief that you failed. Anyway, Ignatius, you can be certain that I shall look into the matter. I shall get to the bottom of it, if it's the last thing I do. I don't intend to let this drop. You, more than anyone in my class, deserve a grammar school place. I perhaps shouldn't say this, but James Johnson and Michael Sidebottom can't hold a candle up to you. You're head and shoulders above them in ability. You're the ablest pupil I have ever taught, Ignatius. I intend to have a word with Mr Griddle and see how your paper was marked.'

'I would rather you didn't do that, miss,' said Ignatius.

'Don't you want to go to the grammar school?' asked the teacher.

'No, miss,' Ignatius replied. 'I don't.'

'No!' gasped Mrs Sculthorpe.

'No, miss, I don't want to go. You see, my father and mother can't afford to send me, what with the uniform and everything else.'

'We could see if you could get some financial help,'

said Mrs Sculthorpe. 'A scholarship or something of that kind. I'm sure –'

'Miss,' interrupted Ignatius, 'even if I did manage to get a scholarship, what happens if my brothers and sisters pass? They probably won't get a scholarship and it would be unfair for me to go to the grammar school and not them. So it's really for the best that I go to the secondary modern.'

'Did you deliberately fail that paper, Ignatius?' asked Mrs Sculthorpe. Ignatius didn't answer. 'You did, didn't you? Oh, Ignatius,' she sighed.

'Things sometimes don't turn out as we might like them to,' said Ignatius, 'but what can anyone do? You must take what life throws at you and make the best of it. I'll be happy enough at the secondary modern. Thank you for all you have done for me, miss. You're a very good teacher and I will miss your lessons.'

'The teachers at the grammar school will never know what they're missing, Ignatius,' said Mrs Sculthorpe. I detected a tremble in her voice.

I have never forgotten that overheard conversation between Mrs Sculthorpe and my very best friend, Ignatius Plunket.

Werner Schmalenbach

(born 1920 at Göttingen) studied Art History at Basle (Dr. Phil.) and was Assistant of the Basle Gewerbemuseums. Is today Director of the Kestner-Gesellschaft in Hanover. As well as the study of different ethnographical and art history subjects, he has influenced an understanding of Modern Art, by contributing to many publications (about Paul Klee, Marc Chagall, etc.) and through large exhibitions of the works of artists of our time.

The Noble Horse

Werner Schmalenbach

The Noble Horse

A journey
through the history of art

Translated from the German
by Daphne Machin Goodall

With a Foreword by
Lionel Edwards, R.I.

1, Lower Grosvenor Place
London S.W.1

First published under the title
Adel des Pferdes
1959
English edition published 1962

PRINTED IN HOLLAND FOR
ROBERT STOCKWELL LTD., LONDON, S.E.I

Contents

The horse in Art through the Ages
Foreword by Lionel Edwards, R.I.

I COMMEND to your notice this book on the Horse as Hero. The beautiful reproductions are well chosen and cover not only an immense period of time but also most of the Earth's surface, with one notable exception of which more anon.

Starting with his cave drawings I feel the author has not given sufficient credit to the handiwork of prehistoric man. These cavemen attempted to depict motion with great simplicity of line and their drawings do suggest both life and movement – which later draughtsmen lost. Although civilisation advanced – the early painters failed to keep up with it. In fact the horse came off rather badly, with some exceptions of course, in the paintings of the Italian Masters. Later the Netherlands produced a considerable number of horse painters. Rubens – whose fat horses rivalled his fat women – depicted the great Flemish horse with some success. Van Dyck's horses are an improved type, still big and heavy, but evidently well 'managed' for he often depicts them in the position of the 'Lavade' (a simple form of Haute École). Gentlemen were very proud of their horsemanship in those days, hence their desire to show off! Velasquez also often painted his patrons in a similar position – although in the illustration of Don Balthasar Carlos, he has altered it into what is often called the 'flying plunge,' in the endeavour to suggest speed.

Art is an elastic term, many critics being of the opinion that animals and art have only the first letter in common. As a painter of horses myself, I am not in their ranks but the author in several passages in this book appears to agree with Aristotle, who said, 'The aim of Art is to represent not the outward appearance of things, but their inward significance. Certainly some of the old (and also of the most modern of these illustrations) depict a quadruped, which has little resemblance to the noble animal.

When we come to more modern times, the French painters seem to have the horse world to themselves, but in Géricault (1821) we first see the influence of the hitherto entirely ignored British school of painters. Géricault's 'Epsom' (the Louvre) is obviously modelled on Herring. It is infinitely better painted, but otherwise Herring all over. Again the colour illustration of a mail coach at an Inn by Agasse, is obviously influenced by Cooper Henderson, the only good painter of horses or vehicles during the coaching era. Jules Louis Agasse was a Swiss who painted in England about 1820. His work is not as well known here as it deserves to be, as there are in England only a few examples, the Swiss Government having collected everything available. There was another painter, James Pollard, who depicted coaches at the same period, but although of historical interest for their meticulous accuracy, they have little artistic value.
The British School of horse painters made a late start as for many years, foreign artists immortalized the equestrian figures of our Kings and aristocracy notably Sir Anthony Van Dyck (1599–1661) who it is said, 'taught the English aristocracy how they ought to look.' Even later we still find a foreign flavour among British horse artists, Agasse was Swiss, Alken a Dane, etc. But the highlights among British horse painters are purely English. Stubbs, whose picture of 'Eclipse' is so well known and to whom the saying, 'Eclipse first and the rest nowhere' might equally have been applied to the artist himself, was born in Liverpool in 1724. He experimented with anatomy at York hospital and lectured to medical students on the subject. His 'Anatomy of the Horse', published in 1776, is highly prized to this day. John Boultbee (1745–1812) was a follower of Stubbs, and is only mentioned as there is in his best work a strong similarity.

Ben Marshall (1767–1835) was apprenticed to Abbott R.A. and excellent though his sporting pictures are – the figures are always better than the horses – which is natural enough as his master was a portrait painter.
John Ferneley (1782–1860), who was apprenticed to Marshall, was a son of a wheelwright at Thrussington. Of humble birth, he was a natural gentleman, and apart from his skill as a painter of horses owed his success to being a good mixer. That his pictures now fetch large figures is chiefly due to the late Major Guy Paget's book, 'The Melton Mowbray of John Ferneley'. There were many other competent painters also, if not quite top of the tree, such as Garrard, James Ward, R.A., Sir Francis Grant, P.R.A., and so on, at more or less the same period.
After these dates there was a long gap with few outstanding painters of the horse until we come to Munnings (1878–1959) who revived the art of horse painting. With him we see a New Art look. Few, if any, of his predecessors attempted to paint the horse in strong sunlight with all the reflections of earth and sky in its satin-like summer coat. Munnings was only the second horse painter to become President of the Royal Academy (Sir Francis Grant being the other). If latterly Munnings became rather mannered and his backgrounds a bit like stage scenery, it is only when he became slightly obsessed with composition and what he called important works that he lost some of the lovely freshness so pleasant in most of his work. But criticise how you will, he still remains the best since Stubbs.
In conclusion, a book of this sort is of great historic value. If it were not for the painters and sculptors of time past, we should know remarkably little about our ancestors.

LIONEL EDWARDS. 1962.

Introduction

THERE ARE many subjects which one could choose as material for a history of art; the portraits of the famous and the unknown would lend distinction to such a theme, and landscape painting would be a pleasant subject if it had appeared in all periods and under all cultures. But, unfortunately, landscape painting denotes a definite period in the development of higher art.

If one looks around for an interesting subject which has appealed to artists from the earliest times, and which has helped to make history, then horses are an obvious choice. There can scarcely be a more pleasant form of travel than riding horses – allowing them to take us at their own comfortable tempo, along the bridleways of art and through the Galleries of Europe.

The horse has been known and admired from time immemorial – by the cave dwellers of pre-history who painted him on their cave walls – to the surrealistic painters of modern times who give him a scarcely recognisable shape. Only a very few great cultures such as the Mexican and Peruvian did not know of horses. The Indians, whom we are unable to imagine without horses, met him for the first time when the Spanish conquered their country; the vision of horse and rider quite took their breath away – they thought both were a single being of divine origin, and it was only when a Spaniard fell off one day that their eyes were opened!

Horses can do for people what nothing else in the world can do – for man is taken completely out of himself once he is mounted. There is nothing which he cannot achieve, he is freed from the controls of space and time. By mounting the horse – and making him a friend and not a slave – man becomes aware of his own power over the animal kingdom and discovers in a very special way the knowledge of human values. In fact, contact with horses teaches one how to cope with one's fellow men!

If we realize this, it does not astonish us that artists of every period have loved horses; and that means they have drawn, painted, sculpted in stone, carved in wood, cast in bronze and modelled them in clay, right down the ages.

We live in an age of speed – mechanized movement in all its shapes and uses – and speed has no use for the leisurely tempo of one of the world's most beautiful and intelligent creatures – a horse in all its nobility!

Nevertheless, if we have time to appreciate art and if we would like to withdraw from the pressure of this industrial age, let us choose the pace of horses, and stop occasionally to admire the work of artists. Let us try to understand the great fascination of an art which has remained unchanged throughout all historical development.

Perhaps, as the reader turns these pages, he will give himself over to quiet and patient meditation. For what really makes the beauty of any one of these pictures of horses, cannot be told, either in many or few words; the language of art, either on horseback or on foot, is untranslatable.

Wild Horse to Riding Horse

LONG BEFORE people rode horses, long before the horse was even harnessed to a primitive plough, at a time when man was neither a farmer nor a cattle-breeder, when he was nothing more than a roving hunter, he had come across the horse. For him, it was a wild animal amongst other wild animals; it meant no more to him than the mammoth and bison, the wild boar or the deer. And so we meet it in the earliest works of art in human history; as a wild animal of the steppes, as game captured forever, by stone-age man on the walls of his caves or on horns and ivory. Magical art? We need not question the exact meaning of these paintings and wall scratchings! Who can really give the answer? However, there cannot be much doubt that they had a cult association.

Probably the animal was not portrayed for the sake of portraiture, but for some other reason. In establishing the animal in effigy – perhaps man tried to capture it. Art could then be a medium of bewitching the hunted animal, and in thus capturing them, perhaps primitive man sought to protect himself from their unforeseen depredations. In this case then, art was a medium of exorcism. We can no longer judge and can only support our explanations by the analogies in the lives of present-day primitive peoples.

However, what is more important than possible solutions for the existence of these artistic representations is that they have nothing magical in themselves; they are neither forced in expression nor symbolically abstract, neither 'expressive' nor 'geometrical' but are perceptive, almost fleeting momentary sketches out of the wild life of the animals; we see here, not supernatural power but appreciation of the power of the animals which man faces with his weapons.

So the wild horses appear in many of the caves in Southern France and Northern Spain; they trot easily in the company of other animals, across the cave walls of Lascaux [1] and on stone-age horns [2], as unself-conscious as people in undisturbed nature, almost a living part of it; with animal characteristics, impressive, but without being burdened by spiritual expression, and with an artistic lightness and verve which – rightly or wrongly – one has called impressionist, almost a reflex upon the eye of the waiting hunter.

DEVELOPMENT went further; man began to cultivate the fruits of the earth, which until then he had only gathered, and to breed the animals which he had hunted. He became a peasant or a cattle-breeder – and much later he became a cattle-owning peasant. At first, flocks and also horses were strange to him, for he lived exclusively from the soil which he cultivated with his own hands, using a spade or hoe; at the most he hunted only as a pastime. So it was once – and so it still is today in most of the primitive cultures of the tropics, especially amongst those peoples who are occupied with figurative art. The cattle-breeder has no art. As a nomad he cannot burden himself with art, especially as he always changes his dwelling-place, and the district in which the spirits of his dead forebears exist.

At this stage of human existence what is art, other than representation of souls, spirits and demons, which one captured in a picture, in order to hold them and make their strength

1 Mural in the caves of Lascaux [Dordogne] Early Stone Age.

useful? For the herdsman that is all; the feeling of oppression through a higher power is unknown; he has nothing to lose and therefore nothing to protect. We see that the primitive peasant cares for his property, and being frightened of demons he prepares to meet the souls of the dead with all sorts of rites and artistic measures. The art which he produces throughout the whole world reflects such oppressions, it is an expression of the spirit world whom it serves. It is expressive art in the highest sense and no longer the optical impression, such as the art of the hunter.

Therefore in the art of primitive peoples one does not come

2 Carving on Deer antler from near Schaffhausen, Switzerland. Early Stone Age.

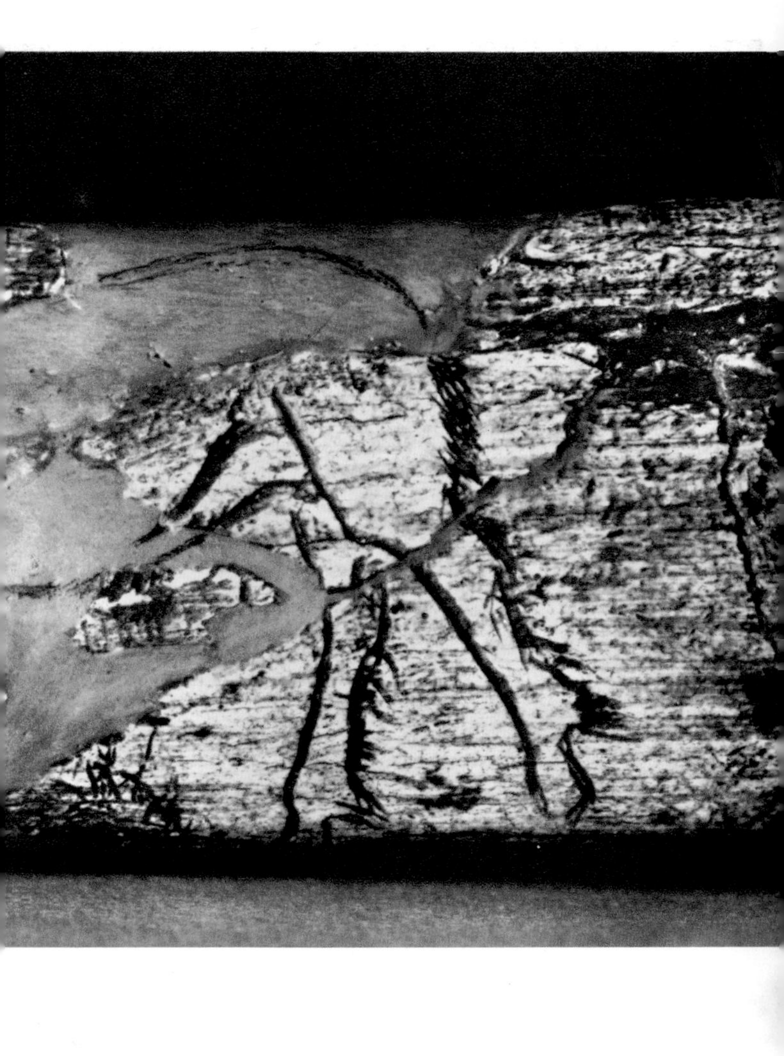

3 Wooden Vase. French Sudan, Africa.

across the horse. The cattle-breeder owned it, naturally, but he did not draw it. The peasant did not reproduce it, because he did not own it. If we see here a negro statue of horses [3] especially one on which a rider appears, it is a rare exception in African art, coming from an area where the central African farmlands bordered the cattle-rich steppes of the Sudan. One need only compare such horses with those of equestrian art in any pastoral culture, to understand that these are working horses which lead a hard life, and not horses which are used to carrying a rider, when man and animal appear to be one.

This is also the case of the rider of Benin [4] although he comes of a quite different and more highly developed culture. The negro countries should not be seen, as is so often the case, as a shapeless unhistorical mass, because there were historical movements of great importance, even high culture, which have sunk again in the course of centuries into the depths of primitive culture.

Thanks to rich artistic finds the culture of the old Benin kingdom of West Africa is the best known to us. At the time of the Renaissance, this kingdom had economic as well as diplomatic relations with the princely houses of Europe, which for their part had commercial establishments, and for a time, embassies in Benin. Then Benin shut itself off more and more against its watchful colonizing neighbours, in the hope of staying the power of the white people. In the year 1897 it was re-discovered during a British punitive expedition. Out of the ruins of the city of Benin which had been razed to the ground, so many hundreds of objects of an old bronze art culture were found, that it gave Europe the opportunity to turn its attention to this art, and especially to negro cultures.

4 Bronze Figure from Benin, West Africa.
5 Ceremonial waggon from Trundholm [Denmark] 1400–1200 B.C.

One was able to observe a skill which could be measured in terms with the much admired workmanship of the highest Oriental and European cultures and which was artistically quite different from primitive wooden idol imagery. But at the same time one was astounded by the fact that in the centre of Africa there were once cultures with all the signs of courtly art; with a characteristic feudalism, a king who was honoured as God at the head, a powerful aristocracy, and a fully developed religion instead of the primitive soul and spirit beliefs. The purpose of these works of art was therefore obviously not the embodiment of spirits and demons, but the representation of terrestrial and supernatural power – the State portrayed; that is the character of this statue of the rider of Benin. With all the insignia and emblems of his power he sits upon a no less representative horse, portraying the unapproachable military clique of the nobility. He does not appear to be 'part of his horse' but as if he had been put on a horse to show what he stood for, not a cavalryman but a much be-weaponed mounted infantryman. For this is no practised rider used to the horse in hunting or war, but just a knight who is riding to a parade. The horse looks 'strange' and he seems to be strange to the man on his back. What was supreme art, was after all grafted on to a 'primitive' peasant culture. The horse served man simply as an hierarchical pedestal, it did not free him from his consciousness of life.

WHERE THE HORSE has become a natural comrade of man and where he begins to take a decisive place in man's way of life – in the pastoral cultures of the world – he does not appear as a motif of art, since pastoral culture has no figurative art. We are therefore unable to observe the horse at the moment when his own art history begins; when the cattle-breeder became lord over the peasant, when the rider became knight, that is

when the horse visibly took his place in the history of art. It is the cattle-owning, horse-owning, weapon-carrying noble who now determines the spirit and style of art, whilst the peasant craftsman only executes the works of art. It is natural that this spirit and style, a free masterful aristocratic spirit, should be different from the former primitive peasant images. The ceremonial chariot from Trundholm [5], Denmark, and the rider's grave-stone of Hornhausen [6], the former, the first in the Germanic Bronze-age and the latter two thousand years later during the migration of nations,* are for Europe the beginning of this development.

The Trundholm chariot points to a further acquisition for mankind, which the owning of cattle and horses bestowed: the wheel. And it is not by accident at this stage of culture – whether in Europe or Asia – that the wheel was not only a means of advancement or movement but also an element of religious ceremonial. It became the symbol of the great constellations Sun and Moon. The one-sided bronze face of the Trundholm chariot, covered with gold leaf, surely represents the face of the Moon. Even in the concentrical circles and spirals of the decorations, the wheel motif occurs again. Above all it is especially noticeable that there is now one supreme

*Trans. note – Began A.D. 250 following the change of climate and the invasion of the Huns A.D. 375 into the east European kingdom of the Germans, e.g. the West Goths through the Balkans to France, Spain and Italy, the East Goths to Italy, the Vandals to Africa, the Allemani, Burgundians and Franks over the Rhine, the Angles and Saxons to Britain, the Langobards to N. Italy, a period of formation of states and present-day Europe – Germany, France England and also the beginning of Russia.

6 Rider's grave-stone of Hornhausen [Saxony]. 8th Cent. A.D.

7 Greek Terracotta. 6 – 5th Cent. B.C.

theme of ornamentation: it is the pastoral language, which is no longer, like the primitive peasant, subjected to the laws of nature on which it was formerly dependent, but itself has now created the laws.

This development is impressively shown by the Hornhausen rider's grave-stone. Here is the proud pastoral squirearchy, well mounted, lifted above the peasant clay, and the earth over which it freely moves is symbolised by a coiled snake ornamentation; the snake – an ancient peasant symbol for the earth – is here a stylized spiralled composition which has lost all its devilishness. This grave-stone comes from the

8 Russian clay toy. 19–20th Cent. A.D.

period of the migration of nations, and from this tremendous fluctuation mediaeval Europe was developed*. Presumably Wotan, the over-lord of the Germanic tribes, is shown here. A very diminutive man, too small, but elevated by the horse on which he sits, he has no body but is joined to the animal by his round shield. The horse is severely stylized with a much too small head on a heavy triangular body – a genuinely noble horse. The work of art, as such, is also full of breeding and nobility, which exemplifies in every line, not so much the natural life of the animal, as the forceful will of the man.

PRIMITIVE FORMS come not only from primitive cultures. In the middle of cultural peaks, even in our time, they recur in the wide sphere which one calls folk art. Forms appear, which could quite as easily have come from ancient times, these are quite outside artistic progress and are related to every epoch of human history. There are small terracotta statues from the Grecian period [7] and clay figures of a later century from southern, western, middle or eastern European countries [8]; it makes no difference whence they originate. Perhaps the dress and headwear are different, perhaps they are objects of religion or toys, but the same artistic simplicity, the same human element unites them into a charming family, which throughout the generations has guarded something tangible of mankind.

*Trans. note – Period of the downfall of the Roman Empire (476) – A.D. 500, until the discovery of America (1492).

The Orient: Horses of State and horses of the Steppes

ABOVE ALL other lands on the earth, Asia can claim to be the native country of the horse. Here, in the vast Steppes of Central Asia it was first tamed and bred; from here it gradually conquered the world. Even our European history, as we learnt at school, shows us repeated invasions by Asiatic steppe riders. There originated, especially in Mesopotamia, the first huge kingdoms of mankind governed by great kings with a powerful system of government, which would remind us of our modern bureaucracy if it had not especially served a god-like monarch and a strong aristocracy. In the development of these kingdoms, in the subjection of the native peasants by mounted conquerors, in the battles of the great to obtain power – the horse played a significant rôle. The ruling classes, whose power became immeasurable, allowed the peasants to use cattle for the cultivation of their fields (this encouraged the 'invention' of the plough and the wheel) but they kept the horse for themselves, and the horse was their most treasured possession. It lent man wings in battle against his enemies, and in the privileged sport of the nobility – hunting. And it was the task of the artists to honour the great in stone. Just as art had been the cult of a higher power, so it became now, even when it belonged to the gods, a political cult, the cult of the great kings of Ur, Assyria, Babylon and Persia, the cult of the Egyptian Pharaoh.

ONE OF OUR pictures shows Assurnasirpal [9], King of the kingdom of Assyria*, on a lion hunt. The chariot driver guides the pair of horses, whilst the king turns backwards to kill a lion growling in pain. A momentary second is held – but held for all eternity: in this second every movement becomes stationary, and the drama an epic. The wheel of the advancing chariot stands still. The horses, which are jumping over a groaning lion, together with the beast of prey form a monumental group and are left motionless by the

*Trans. note – Assur, capital of Assyria, 1400-884 B.C. Assurbanipal, Assyrian King 668-628 B.C., conquered Babylon 648, founded great library (of clay tablets) in the capital Nineveh.

9 Assyrian Relief. Lion Hunt, King Assurnasirpal. 9th. Cent. B.C.

chisel, timeless, almost heraldic figures. Everything is held with great strength; even the moment itself, is at the same time motionless and yet remains extremely alive: the dramatic action of the whole is in the movement of each figure – the leg muscles or the quiet nervosity of the horses' heads. Part of another Assyrian relief [10] shows this even more clearly; it shows, too, not only the illusion of reality but that sculpture also played its part.

THE ASSYRIANS have no equals to compete with them, in the modelling of horses and wild animals, in the great feudal cultures of the old Orient. Even the Egyptians cannot rival them in this respect. Perhaps it is because the horse appeared rather late in Egypt, towards the end of the Middle Dynasty* and the inhabitants of the Nile valley were not so used to him as those of the lands of the Euphrates and Tigris. It came at a period in which art had already begun to become softer, more elegant, even decadent. It came to a country in which there was little but its great river, bordered on both banks by the desert, and there were no steppes, where the ownership of a horse might have meant something. So the horse was only the outer attribute of the monarch. Rameses II, who allows himself to be drawn by a pair of elegant horses in a war chariot, across the wall of a Theban temple [11], has not in the least the inner greatness of an ordinary throned Pharaoh of the old Dynasty nor has he the force of the Assyrian king, who with more barbaric wildness – although the reliefs shown here are of a later period than the Egyptian – leaps into a fight with a hunted lion.

It cannot be denied: Pharaoh's stallions remind us, with their graceful beauty, the rhythmic action of their trot and the nodding plumes on their heads, of the over-bred high school horses of our circus arenas. Similarly – on another relief – in the same style Rameses III is shown in a composition comparable to the Assyrian relief of the lion battle, but the horses and the lions have lost all strength and life: they are mere requisites of royal power, which the sovereign has ordered to be placed on the façade of his temple. Incomparable as is the contribution of the Egyptians to the history of art, it did not encompass the art history of the horse. This is continued within the sphere of Greece in Mediterranean culture.

*Trans. note – Egyptian Middle Dynasty 2040-1710 B.C.

10 Assyrian Relief. 7th. Cent. B.C.

11 *Egyptian Relief from Thebes. New Empire. 13th Cent. B.C.*

ALMOST NO ART has captured the horse with such indescribable liveliness as the east Asian. Here, above all things, the horse is a horse. He is not a parade horse, not even some sort of horse used by man for an especial purpose, but he is something completely natural. Even where a rider forces him into an unnatural gait, one feels that the nature of the animal resists, that the horse gathers his strength against this unfamiliar will, that he concentrates on himself: he has his own will. That is already true of the well-known horse representations of the early Han-Dynasty, which are to be seen on the gravestone reliefs of that very worthy family Wu [12] in the year 168 B.C. There we find movement, even in a severely composed design of battles and hunts, processions and dances, clowns and domestic scenes. From their appearance the horses represent the dominion and splendour of the great. It would almost seem from the size of them that they express the riches and independence of their owner. They are all pictured after a single scheme. But the scheme has no rigidity; the horses' bodies are full of life, combined with grace and power, with their majestic quietness; their powerfully built frames, their exquisitely fine limbs, their snorting nostrils, they are ready, with all speed to conquer and win.

There are no limitations to the number of horse representations during the course of Chinese art, and the variety of motifs throughout the centuries is as inexhaustible as Nature itself. So we have innumerable terracottas from the best period of Eastern Asiatic history, perhaps the most beautiful from the T'ang Dynasty epoch [13] and we have numberless ink drawings and wood-cuts. What a contrast to the horses of the old imperial kingdoms of the near East! There, we have monumental eminence, immortalized in stone, here, momentary fleeting movement; there, personal even political greatness, here, pure nature which embraces humanity just as it does horses and trees.

BUT IT IS NOT only the unique feeling for the natural and the living which East Asia allows us to catch so intimately. It is – with this closely-woven feeling for Nature – a quite definite artistic principle. At the top in the hierarchy of the Arts, the Asiatic places the written word which is cultivated in its purest sense. In that the scribe uses the same word-sign again and again, he seeks to plunge himself into meditation on the significance of the world. All personal will and desire, all personal fate is overcome in writing, and the moment of 'enlightenment' is sought in which the personal combines with the universal; the written work, the brush-work, is but a drawing of breath. In reality, by writing he tries to overcome all life's worthlessness and to achieve harmony with Nature, to be a part of her. In this the sage of the Far East finds the highest spiritual freedom. The horse of Itcho Hanabuse [14] has complete freedom of character drawn into it as if the artist is only the medium of self-acknowledged Nature. Even so, it is not an ink drawing but a wood-cut, which normally by its freedom of style would tend toward rough forms; here the whole directness of a flowing handwriting is retained. Only the horse's lines are shown, and yet no muscle, no physical roundness, no single additional typical detail could give a more suggestive impression of a living horse.

12 *Chinese Relief Tablet, from the grave of the Wu family. Han-Dynasty. 168 A.D.*

13 *Chinese Terracotta. T'ang-Dynasty. A.D. 10th Cent.*

14 *Japanese Wood-cut by Itcho Hanabuse. About 1700.*

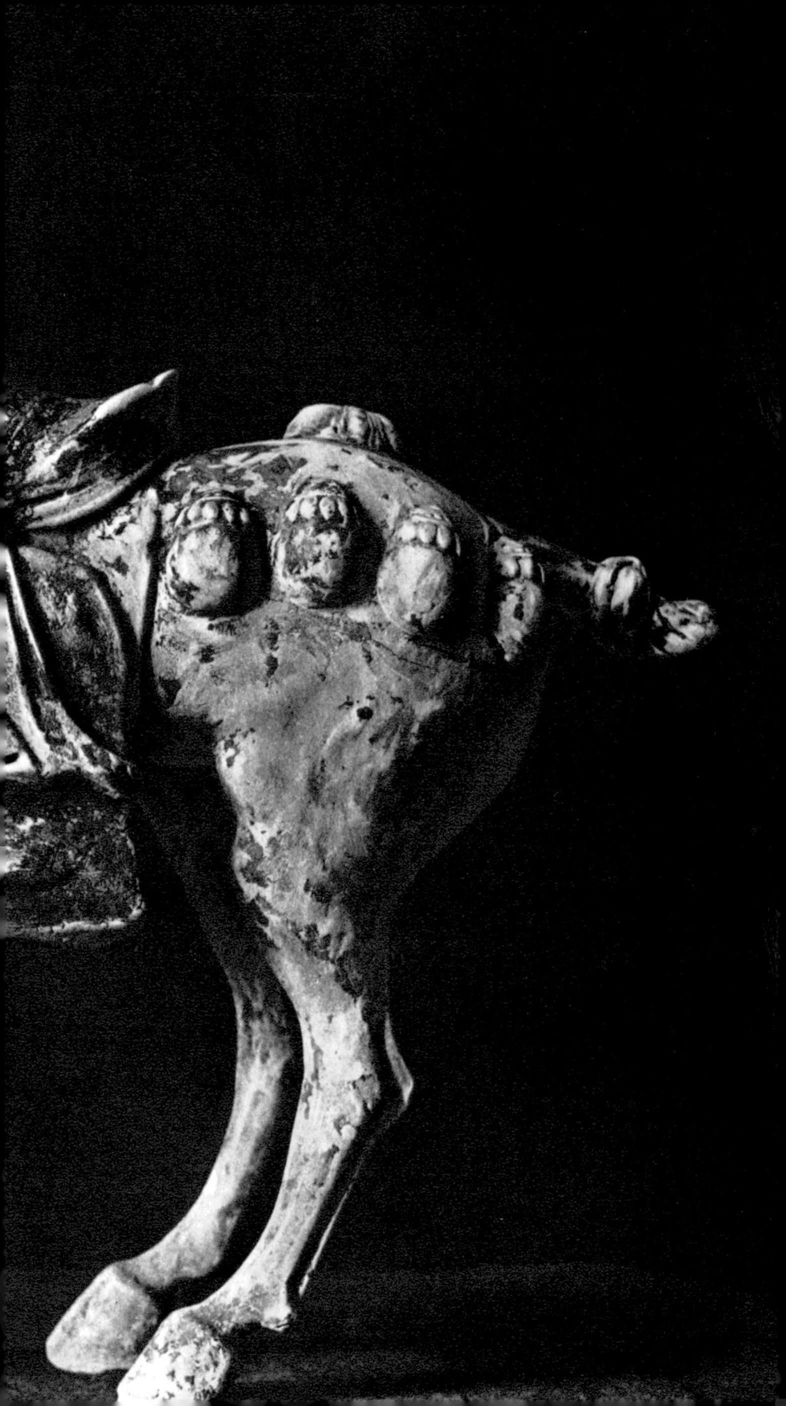

15 Part of a Greek vessel. 8th Cent. B.C.

Horses of Greek citizens and Roman emperors

FOR A LONG PERIOD European intellect and art had set the absolute criterion in the creation of classical Greece. 'Hellas' was equally significant in that fifth century before Christ, in which the people of Athens raised the sanctuary of the Acropolis as we see it today: that Greece of the classical era which the Persians had conquered and which had freed itself from the powerful grip of the Orient. It is here that the history of the Occident begins. Athens of the fifth century had the same influence as that Athens of the mature goddess Pallas Athene, who emerged from the head of Zeus. As one looks back at the early cultures of the earth and allows oneself to be charmed by their evidence, then early Greek art has contributed a very great deal. It belongs, as a matter of course, to the great and quite invaluable history of plastic art.

At one time Hellas was over-run by cavalcades of riders from the North, and the centuries-long contact with the inhabitants whom they subjugated, produced Greek culture. The songs of Homer tell us of these legendary times. The same spirit of these heroic sagas is mirrored in the funeral vessel [15] of the early Greek period, which one may term geometrical after its artistic form. Cavalcades of riders are shown – horse-drawn chariots, solemn funeral processions in which the distinguished dead, laid out on top of the bier, are seen drawn by horses accompanied by wailing men and women. The large surface of the vase is divided into panels and friezes; geometrical ornamentation fills every space and people and animals are drawn to abstract forms. A forceful masculine art, in which the self-gratification of a free humanity, as it became centuries later, is unknown; but it is also no longer subjected to extravagant authority of a god-like master: Man has become the standard of all things and this standard is applied to the horse. This is not the language of the Orient. In all this ceremonial there prevails a serene and wonderful lightness which would never have been thought of, in the old Oriental cultures; and there also prevails an unmistakable rhythmic feeling for form in which one may notice the possibility of a splendid development.

It is certainly an aristocratic rather than a homely art. And now representative and authoritative political art is no more. The refined individual is dependent upon himself and the society of his equals. When he gets into his quadriga [16] he is not a great king, and these are not his vassals; he is a free Greek noble and he has created the Greek gods after his own image. The black-figured Quadriga on a dish of the 6th century is full of this independent aristocratic spirit. But like the horses, the style is subdued. The horses obey not only the charioteer but also the unalterable rule of art. They are still pictured after a uniform scheme and their position is as symmetrical as a coat of arms. But life flows from their graceful bodies. In spite of stylistical restraints they are nervous, lively animals, eager to race. And already, with great care, the surface has been broken through: the future softly issues a challenge and an artistic theme arises which will occupy artists for many centuries and will also often mislead them. Obviously the horses and the man turn their heads sideways because of the confined surface. But the connection is still intact – the artistic and the social. There is not yet a

16 Attic dish. Quadriga. 6th Cent. B.C.

completely free rein; a memory still remains of that time when cavalry invaded the land and put themselves over the peasants. It is symbolized here – compare it with the rider of Hornhausen – by the division of an upper and lower region: the earth-snake under the feet of the victorious chariot driver.

GREEK HISTORY has a faster heart-beat than that of the old Orient. In the same century as the Quadriga, although towards the end, the charming vase-picture of Euphronios [17] was created. Shortly before the red figure technique overtook the black in Greek vase painting, that is to say – the style of silhouetting which was depicted only by the medium of line drawing, was followed by a style which allowed physical details and natural positions to be followed in free-hand. The entire style has become more liberal. The youth sits easily and naturally on the horse's back. Even if he appears to smile somewhat formally – it is the famous 'archaic smile' – and so he goes his way laughing, giving expression to a fresh warm feeling of life. The horse prances, free from any sort of forced style, with a rhythmic contour within the confines of the vase. And in the place of the festiveness of the old Quadriga, a certain 'Sunday' feeling has appeared*. Now individual names are given. The description shows that the youth is called Leargos and because of his beauty, is being fêted, and the painter who signs the work of art with his name is called Euphronios. As we know, quite a number of the most beautiful Grecian vases have come from his hand. How very much to the fore the personalities of the artists now appear, is shown in a rather naive manner by the inscription on the

*Trans. note – Especially German 'to have a Sunday feeling', Sunday being a special day.

17 Inside picture of dish of Euphronios.
510 B.C.

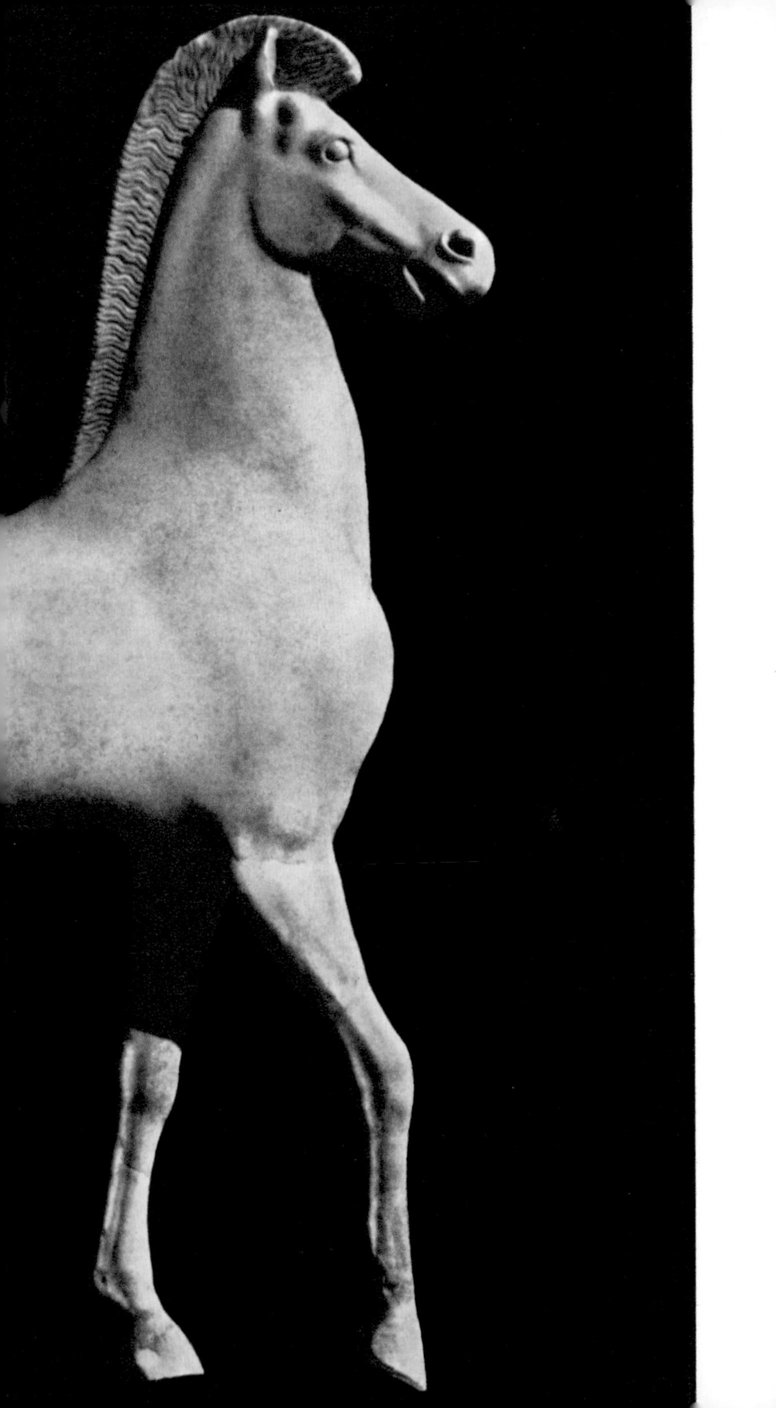

18 Marble horse from the 'Persian Ruins' of the Acropolis, Athens, 490–480 B.C.

vase of a no less praiseworthy rival of Euphronios, where his mortification appears in the lines: 'Painted by Euthymides, in a way which Euphronios would never have achieved'. This inscription points to a wider sense of newly-won freedom; freedom of economical competition, in which a master potter has to maintain his position against others.

IN THE YEAR 480 the Persians conquered Athens and were on their way, unknowingly, to their severest defeat. They occupied and destroyed the town and the temple buildings on the Acropolis. But quite soon they were completely beaten by the Greeks and the Acropolis arose in new splendour. The sculptures damaged by the Persians were buried in the earth, where they remained for over 2,000 years until they were re-discovered in 1884 in the so-called 'Persian ruins', amongst them the lovely marble sculpture of a horse, which the picture [18] shows. This horse has the same nobility as that of the horses of both vase paintings. He is full of characteristic vigour, and at the same time full of 'deportment'. In him the people of Athens have erected a memorial, as in those statues of the youths and maidens which were buried with him. If humanity had the standard of these people, one could also say that its standard was the horse, so much was it on the same level as the people themselves. That is what this horse radiates; the same freedom, the same pride and the same natural nobility. The characteristics of 'aliveness' and eagerness with the forefoot stamping, lightly and gracefully, have prevailed over the size of the body. He was not only used, but loved and respected by man: a comparative glance backwards to the Assyrian reliefs makes one feel that this horse, these people – and this spirit must, in the end, be victorious over the power and might of the Orient.

EVERY FOURTH year the citizens of Athens celebrated the

feast of their city's goddess, Athene. They went in festive processions, priests and notabilities, on foot and on horseback, with chariots, sacrificial animals and offerings up to the Temple hill, to pay homage to the goddess from the town which was under her protection. This gay procession is shown on the Parthenon, the Temple of Athene on the Acropolis. In a spread of about one hundred and sixty metres* the wonderful frieze encircles the Temple, in a loose yet firmly bound grouping. Today the greater part is to be found in museums. Instead of the almost martial formation of Egyptian sacrificial processions, in which the individual was only a link in a nameless chain, there appears the rhythmical coming and going of people who have made their own standards for social behaviour. And the throned Olympic gods await the procession, not as super-men but simply as distinguished citizens of Athens.
There lies a long road between the exceptionally stylised battle horses of the early times and the horses of the classic period as they appear on the Parthenon frieze [19], the road of

*Trans. note – 1 metre = 39 inches.

19 Part of the Pathenon Frieze from the Acropolis, Athens. Middle 5th Cent. B.C.

the old Greek kingdoms to the civil democracies of the fifth century. These horses of the Parthenon are no longer formal drawings as were the horses on the 'geometrical' vases, but real horse personalities. They are rather to be compared with those of the Chinese – complete horses, all temperament, living for themselves, controlled by the restraining will of man without giving up their own lively nature; they keep their fire even when they have to obey the measured rhythm of a lively procession. In the Far East Nature dominated and included horse and man together, but here the human will and spirit are dominant. If the horses are appreciated there with a secret intuition, so, in this case man stands apart from Nature as a precise observer and at the same time the guardian of an ideal of beauty and inward bearing, which he has imposed upon himself and all things. Now the single parts of the animal's body are considered important – muscles, veins, conformation, surface. To use a simple expression; the representations have become naturalistic, whilst in the East Asiatic's art, they are natural but never naturalistic. This naturalism includes as a matter of course idealism – neither have yet split apart – as they are soon to do. This pairing of nature and ideas, of truth and beauty, is the whole essence of Greek classical art.

And here, too, a name has been handed down to us, that of the great master of classical times: Phidias. He is responsible for the Parthenon sculptures, even though they were executed by other hands. Although Euphronios could be named, he had scarcely the individuality of a tangible handworker to us, but here, in Phidias, we have before us one of the first great artists. Now the history of art begins to speak in the names of artists. More especially if the individual is one with the community, he then accepts responsibility. He is no longer the anonymous craftsman amongst craftsmen but the artist. From now on artist personalities with their names and their fates will appear in the light of posterity.

THIS WORLD came to a close in endless civil wars, to make way for a new and completely changed one – that Hellenistic world, the Greece of the victorious Alexander the Great. Now it was the Greeks who went off to conquer distant lands and achieve world power; and it was they who fell upon the kingdom of Persia, under the leadership of their young Macedonian king. This renewed and combined reflection of

20 *Piece from the Alexander Mosaic. Roman copy from 'House of the Faun' in Pompeii after a late Greek painting.*

Orient and Occident has been retained in the Roman mosaic copy of a Greek painting of the Hellenistic period – the mosaic of the 'Battle of Alexander' [20] which once decorated the well-known 'House of the Faun' in Pompeii, and is today admired by tourists in the museum at Naples. The battle between the two opposite armies is shown with unequalled brilliance. In the midst of battle, Alexander and the Persian king Darius come face to face – the latter's chariot is already turned to flee. So everything is concentrated upon a most dramatic moment. The calm peace of the fifth century is shattered for all time. Here the value lies in rapid movement, in passionate excitement, in Alexander's fiery glance, and in the flaring eye of the attacking horse; that is the language of Hellenistic art.

IT IS NOT very often that in Hellenistic times art rose to a height such as that which produced the splendid bronze horse whose torso was found in the neighbourhood of Cape Artemision [21]. This 'noble simplicity and quiet greatness', which was once praised by Winckelmann* that great admirer of Greek art, has no equal. The nobility and the 'breed' of the horse are no longer in question, but his physical capabilities must be considered. Such a speed would never have been credited to the horses of the Acropolis – neither

*Trans. note – Founder of the study of classical art A.D. 1717-68.

before nor after its destruction by the Persians. There, one would never have met a horse over whose back one hears the crack of a whip. The greatest physical effort is being demanded from this animal, without attention to the balance of nature and imagination by which classical art was ruled. And since this has been done with great care for construction, it is an exception in the art of this period and is evidently the comprehensive work of an exceptional artist. Because the spirit of the classical era, which held naturalism and idealism together, was broken, free scope was given to an obtrusive naturalism which reproduced only reality. In the place of idealism there appeared a noticeable shallow pathos. And this inglorious artistic method was continued by Rome.

ROMA NON CANTAT – Rome cannot sing. Rome was not an artistic nation, but a political nation seeking world power of the first order. So the horse once more returns to his old Oriental function. He is now a state horse, a parade horse, an object for representational purposes, no longer in the old controlled artistic language, but in the language of naturalism freed of all repressions. Natural and supernatural forms broke away from each other. For all the coming centuries this was such a fateful break, that today any naturalistic step is regarded by us as a step backward – and thus we do many an old work of art an injustice. But let us not anticipate!

NOT BEAUTY, but size; not form, but greatness! This is shown by one of the grandest works of Roman sculpture, the statue

21 Bronze Horse from Cape Artimision. Middle 2nd Cent. B.C.

22 *Bronze Statue of the Emperor Marcus Aurelius on the Roman Capitol. 2nd half of the 2nd Cent. A.D.*

of the Emperor Marcus Aurelius on the Roman Capitol [22]. It is the 'father' of all subsequent equestrian portraiture, and is equalled by none of them. Of course one should not look for the details, the bridle, saddle, sandals, and muscles; and the absence of much will strike those who come fresh from looking at Grecian equestrian statues. The carriage alone is overpowering, the internal as well as the external; overpowering, too, is this enormous, magnificently patinated bronze mountain of a horse; and as everyone who stands in front of it knows – a world Empire was ruled with this gesture. It is a symbol of the tremendous power of the Roman Empire.

Middle Ages: the horse under the Sign of the Cross

IN THE MIDDLE AGES the heir to Roman world power was the Christian Church, and the heir to the Roman Emperor was the Pope who resided in the Holy City. As the God of the poor and suffering, Christ rode to Jerusalem on an ass's back. Thus, with the ascent of the spiritual conquest of the world, the horse was displaced from his high position as a medium of expression of worldly dominion. Worldly splendour, to which the beauty of the horse belonged, was out-shone by the immortal splendour of Christian revelation.

Was this a bad time for the horse? Quite the contrary, for the Middle Ages saw the flowering of European chivalry. Out of the rider of antiquity, the knight appeared. The Middle Ages are full of horses, full of cavalry battles and mounted games. They found their finest expression in the great tournaments. We meet this worldly, courtly culture and with it the horse, in the art of the period, even if only on the edge, because art was only for the serious service of the Church. Therefore the horse remained a rather strange motif. It had no place in the Cathedrals, and only a very few themes found a place for it, such as John's vision of the riders of the Apocalypse, the Three Magi from the East, the knightly St. Martin and St. George and a few other legendary and visionary figures.

For the people of the Middle Ages, all things and beings of this world had meaning only so far as they proclaimed the

Honour of God and His Works. In themselves they were nothing. So the artist showed them not as material reality but as an expression of supernatural spirituality. Their mortal splendour was taken from them as if it were an outer garment. Everything was given up which antiquity in its free impetuosity had conquered – organic aliveness amounting almost to activity, anatomical exactitude, spaciousness within perspective – in short, correctness within the meaning of naturalism. But they gained immeasurably thereby: Art never lost itself again in the banalities of reality but became the expression of human, personal experience. It was the expression above all of Christian belief and was ruled by a precept which followed its own laws and no longer those of an external nature.

HOW FAR REMOVED is the horse of one of the Apocalyptic riders in the 'Bamberger Apocalypse' [23] – one of the finest miniatures of the romantic Middle Ages – from all the horses of Greek-Roman antiquity! It is not alive in the sense that it has its own life; it is even grotesque with anatomical faults; but just this disproportion in the stilted way he appears, is an amazing piece of formal audacity, of an artistic expressiveness and beauty which has no equal – an ugly horse if one looks at him physically, but a lovely horse if one looks at him as a work of art. In the rider one sees the resemblance to the tradition of late antiquity, but his Christian faith robs him of his Roman pride. Look at the shy way his right hand holds the arrow, not self-confidence, but confidence in eternity gives him – even in his helplessness – an expression of greatness and physical strength.

THE HORSES of the Magi appear twice as a group of three, without their riders, on one of the best preserved works of romanesque monumental painting – the wooden screen in

23 Apocalyptic Rider from the 'Bamberg Apocalypse'. About 1000 A.D.

the Church of Zillis in Grisons [24]. This screen divided into 153 quadratical panels, dates to the first half of the twelfth century, but it is in the style of the eleventh century, which lasted longer in the isolated Alpine districts than in the then centres of art. These pictures were painted for the peasants, and they are the result of peasant intelligence. Thus their style preserves a certain provincial archaism which does their greatness no harm. On the contrary, it is simply in this that a large part of their strength and expressiveness lies. The greater crudity of contrast to that of other works of Romanesque painting, in which the melancholic is mixed with rural joy makes this picture especially admirable. The three horses stride comfortably on to the scene. They are not so well bred as the horses in the 'Bamberger Apocalypse'. Their heavy heads nod as if they were pulling a plough, and they lift their legs as if they had some difficulty in pulling them out of the soil. The horses are built on a grand scale covering a great area into the archway. Strong black lines divide them and give the details, always in sweeping strokes, but also controlled, even if the horses are somewhat crowded into the ornamental framework. The artist appears to have a ready form for every detail, a formula which he paints in like the letters of a drawn hand-writing; certain formulas for jaw, eyes, ears, hair, legs and hooves. It is the language of old parchment illustration, turned into the prodigious.

RETURNING FROM the screen of Zillis to the Persian-Byzantine* silk material [25], one steps not only a few centuries back, but back into a sphere of a greater worldliness and 'international' art, in which the Orient and the Occident shared. In the year A.D. 313 the Emperor Constantine the Great recognised Christianity in the Edict of Milan. He had further designated the city of Byzantium as the capital of the the Roman Empire instead of Rome. Byzantium and Rome were still held in *one* hand, but they were soon to part, politically and religiously. Byzantium grew in importance and it developed, thanks to its unique position on the

*Trans. note – Persian Dynasty 226 B.C.-A.D. 651

24 *Panel from the Church Screen, Zillis [Grisons] The horses of the Magi. 1st half 12th Cent.*

25 Byzantine Copy of the 6th to 8th Cent. after a Sassanian silk material.

Bosphorus, into a place of convergence for economical as well as spiritual intercourse between East and West. All the merchant routes to Europe from the Near and also the Far East led through the city, which became the richest and most flourishing of the Middle Ages. Both Asia and Europe stamped it. The silk material pictured here displays its world-wide connections; though probably of Byzantine origin, it is in any case the reproduction of Sassanian and therefore Persian work. The Sassanian ruled over Persia as a dynasty from the third century until they were put aside by the Arabic invasions of the seventh century. At that time Sassanian works of art poured to the West in rich measure; amongst them costly silk materials like this one, were traded in Byzantium and so came to Italy and Northern Europe. Here they were put to the use of the Church possibly as reliquary garments – heathen things put to Christian use. Obviously East and West share our material. The rider has unmistakable traces of late Roman-early Christian human portrayal, such as we recognise in the Copts in Egypt or Byzantium, the same lack of body, the same expression which is especially shown in the wide-open eyes which are not focused upon this world. At the same time, we see the signs of Oriental art: the heraldic composition, the armorial animal groups, the ornamental motif; the subject of a royal rider charging a lion – shown here attacking a wild ass – which at a distance reminds us of the reliefs of old Mesopotamia; and lastly there is the significance of the scene, which shows the Sassanian Prince Bahram Gor of the fifth century.

THE PORTRAYAL of people, horses and almost everything visible, changes in the course of the peak period of the Middle Ages, in the course of the Gothic period from generation to generation in the accomplishment of a quite definite

26 Mounted statue in Bamberg Cathedral. About 1240.

aim, which was, of course, only completely achieved in the Renaissance; this was the accomplishment of naturalism, through which animals and men regained their autonomy. A significant step in this direction, in the middle of the Gothic period, was marked by the Bamberg and Naumberg sculptures. Here, man appears in complete possession of his worldly strength and even if a ray from Beyond strikes him, it does not change his physical appearance. So the rider of Bamberg [26] stands before us – a worldly rider, the epitome of his century, the classic representation of Mediaeval knighthood. Christian faith shining from his countenance does not yet allow this body free development. Nature still appears transfigured through Christianity, but no longer suppressed, not over-powered. It is only controlled, ennobled by inward deportment. The horse, magnificent animal though he is, has a certain stiffness; so has no character in himself, and is only the bearer of the man waiting patiently until he feels the spur.

TWO MORE PICTURES of real mediaeval chivalry now appear with a richer, more perceptive medium of portrayal, Pisanello's 'Vision of St. Eustace' [27] and the equestrian picture of Guidoriccio by Simone Martini [28], both paintings by two great artists of the Italian late Middle Ages. Everything which Naturalism characterises is again attempted, without the ban being completely broken. In Pisanello's picture it is as if Nature was suddenly awakened to a flowering life, having been freed from its Mediaeval sleep. But the animals still spread themselves timorously into the landscape; it does not accept them as a matter of course. In Simone Martini's work horse and scenery are divided one from the other, the landscape remains in the wings, and the rigid position in profile of horse and rider is a sign that the com-

27 Antonio Pisano [Pisanello]. Vision of St. Eustace. About 1440.

plete break-through to freedom from all limitations of faith and courtly ceremony has not yet taken place.

LET US TRANSFER ourselves once more to Asia. The late Court art of mediaeval Occident is comparable, in every way, to the late Court art of India and of Mohammedan Persian culture. The Persian miniature [29] from 'Shah Nameh' from 'The Book of Kings' comes from the same fourteenth century, as do both our last equestrian paintings. If it were not for the scarcely noticeable characteristics of a

28 *Simone Martini, portrait of the General, Guidoriccio dei Fogliani da Reggio [part.].*

29 *Persian Miniature, middle 14th Cent.*

strange nationality, the miniature could be the portrayal of a European Tournament of the early Middle Ages. And how nearly related in every other particular, to the picture of 'Guidoriccio' is the picture of 'Said Khan' [30] which belongs to a much later period – the seventeenth century! There, too, the spirit of an over-refined Court culture is shown – a horse carrying out his representative duty, which is performing a 'High School' movement, rider and horse in severe profile and in perceptible restraint as opposed to unrestricted Natural-

ism. Up to a point everything, even the magnificent stallion, is more true to life – not that this means that it is more beautiful! – than the one in Simone Martini's picture: the rider sits completely at ease with his whole weight in the saddle, as one may also say of the earlier riders of our Persian miniature. But the personal self-confidence is not, as with the Christian knight, weighted down with care for the Beyond. It is the self-confidence of the Asiatic rider of knightly estate, for no sort of humility is required by Islam, and he remains undisturbed and in possession of his whole strength.

30 Indian Miniature. Portrait of Said Khan, Ruler of Khabul. 17th Cent.

Renaissance and Baroque:* Parade horses and plough horses

A NEW PERIOD OF Occidental history begins about 1400. To the people, the artists of the Renaissance, this secular reform was deeply and proudly appreciated and today we know that this epoch brought with it a style, which we choose to call modern, as opposed to the mediaeval. The pressure of mediaeval authority, worldly as well as spiritual, has given way and has left Nature free. Not that the Christian faith has been shaken, but it no longer presses upon outward reality: even when it is serving God's work, it lies bereft of all enchantment, but is itself enchanting in the eyes of mankind. Themes from heathen mythology are now allowed, even loved, without anyone in any way believing in the Olympic gods: not faith but humanity and beauty are now the deciding factors. A new classic has been achieved having arrived at maturity through a great example – classical antiquity. It cannot be told here how this came about, how courtly ceremonial of the Middle Ages was overthrown by civic merchants and craftsmen, how cities became more and more the decisive factor governing art. At first it was in the small-town manner of the late Gothic style and early Renaissance, then in the wider distinguished civic sense of high Renaissance. Art is no longer in the completely limited service of

*Trans. note – Baroque style of art etc. followed the Renaissance in the 16th century, lasted in Europe until the middle of the 18th century.

God, but devoted to the outside occasions of this world, to the attraction of worldly destinies, to all the beauty upon which the eyes may faest. In the beginning, with a truly botanical perception the artist studied each and every detail and idealized it in the maturity of complete inner freedom, combined with a new ambition to give reality a higher ideal. So on the one hand we have Naturalism and on the other Idealism – the human ethos, the glorification of spiritual values. And then once again after the culmination of a few

31 Paolo Uccello. Rout of San Romano 1456/60.
32 Benozzo Gozzoli. Procession of the Magi. About 1460.

decades, both will separate: Naturalism will have difficulty in expressing Idealism, until the artists decide to follow fresh paths.

TO THE MASTERPIECES of the fifteenth century belong three abundantly illustrated horse pictures of battle-fields, by the great Florentine painter Paolo Uccello to be found in the

galleries of Florence, Paris and London [31]. One needs to look back only to Antonio Pisanello or Simone Martini, to realise that a new era has appeared. Nature has complete mastery. If it were necessary to conquer her, step by step, this undertaking has no other purpose but to overpower her pictorially. Scarcely any other painter has undertaken this task with as much strength as Uccello. It was the 'scientific' problem of anatomy and, above all, of perspective with which the artist was occupied – and more than occupied; he was passionately devoted to it and because of it these pictures were far more than scientific exercises. Every shortening of perspective and transversion of subject matter has a dramatic place for Uccello, and his charmingly eager way of painting in multifarious details between the horses' legs gives depth to his canvas. Of course the 'free' canvas space is not yet closed up; everything still takes place upon a stage in the foreground with which the landscape in the background has but little connection. But apart from the actual scene, the space left by the twisting and turning horses, and by riders and fallen is richly taken up with helmets and weapons which have dropped to the ground.
With the strength and passion in which everything is painted, an extraordinary sense of clarity and monumental greatness of composition are blended together. Such a huge battle-action had not been seen by art since the Graeco-Roman Mosaic of Alexander.
COMPARED WITH these pictures, the frescoes with which Benozzo Gozzoli, who was twenty years younger than Uccello, decorated the private chapel of the Medici [32] appear like a return to the Mediaeval. Although they give him the same problems of natural reproduction as those which were presented to his great compatriot, he shows nothing of Uccello's

33 Leonardo da Vinci. Silverpoint drawing for a memorial for Francesco Sforza. About 1485.

tempestuous perception and nothing of his great spirit. In spite of all the truthful details a certain enchantment lies over Nature. And in everything else the retarded temperament of the painter is shown – in the overflow of material riches, in the formality of the trees and especially in the stage by stage scenery, in the rocky tracks where we see an approaching cavalcade, led by the Magi dressed in Florentine

34 Hans Baldung [Grien]. Sleeping Stable Boy and the Witch. Wood-cut 1544.

fashion, with the two Princes Cosimo and Lorenzo de Medici at the head.

A FEW YEARS previous to 1500 we have Leonardo's silverpoint sketch for a statue of Francesco Sforza, Duke of Milan [33]. The fate of the Middle Ages is sealed by this drawing, once and for all. A free confident humanity once more bestrides the horse. A glance at the drawing allows one to understand, that for these people, the Middle Ages must appear as a dismal interval between happier periods. Here is a revival of the classical human ideal of antiquity, its artistic ethos: and if Leonardo's fiery steed has a resemblance to anything then it is to the horses of the Parthenon frieze on the Acropolis in Athens. Here, too, Leonardo gives us a living horse, full of life, wonderfully proportioned, noble and well-bred in every line but in no way degenerate, Nature and sensual understanding are in complete harmony. So one might imagine, with slight differences, were the designs which Phidias made for the Parthenon horses nearly two thousand years earlier!

SUCH A FEELING of fluid and happy naturalness was not known by the painters of the German high Renaissance with perhaps the exception of Hans Holbein. What the Italians accomplished as unproblematical, remained a problem for the Germans right through the fifteenth century. An artist like Hans Baldung, creator of the wood-cut of a sleeping stable-boy [34], had difficulty in expressing naturalism. He meant to show a natural horse; but it remains a study of anatomy and perspective. And with the stable-boy he is captured quite obviously, more by the audacious shortening of perspective and the materialism of the dress than by the personal subject. The compass of the picture is not freed from the grip of construction; it is less a stable than a stereometrical hollow space, so that one is not surprised to meet

·H·B·

35 Albrecht Dürer. Knight, Death and the Devil. Engraving 1513.

decorative volutes which are rather unusual in a stable. Nature is just put aside for scientific study: man and animal are sacrificed to the demands of space and anatomy, the stable is similarly relegated to unimportance in a central perspective building up of space. And yet such a page has a great artistic charm, which lies in the significance of its representation, in the mastery of the wood-cut technique, and lastly in the character of the artist. It is not an unreal purely 'theoretical' picture. One might also say that something is retained of the reality of the peasants' war*, which broke out at this time.

DÜRER'S WELL-KNOWN engraving 'Knight, Death and the Devil' [35] must not be left out. If it is greater and grander than Baldung's wood-cut, the greatness is gained not through lack of detail: Naturalism allows no single, minute and meaningless detail to be left out. The finest and most complete method of engraving is used for this infinite exactitude. Only Albrecht Dürer's artistic genius prevents the horse and other figures from being made up of multiplied units: they are *really* all of a piece. But with all the beauty of this composition the separation of naturalism and a higher idealism is already noticeable: the over-natural, allegorical motif is basically not suitable for naturalistic representation. The picture produces rather an effect of a cavalcade of dressed-up figures than a valid symbol. So here strikingly effective is the tragedy of Naturalism which Leonardo's sketch avoids, thanks to its lightness and draughtsmanship. This tragedy will come later to tragi-comedy, to lack of taste and piled-up trumpery

*Trans. note – Rebellion of central and south German peasants 1524-25.

S 1513

of centuries. But even now it overshadows a great master. To perceive this, one needs only to give oneself over to the impression created by the powerful horse. In spite of the abundance of detail, the play of the muscles, the change from light to shade, one realises by the exactitude of the wrinkles and of the hair of mane and tail that it is an artistically great horse of the same character and origin as that of Leonardo da Vinci.

THE TWO classical equestrian statues of the Italian Renaissance are well-known – Donatello's 'Gattamelata' in Padua [36] and Verocchio's 'Colleoni' in Venice [37]. Both are 'descendants' of the Emperor Marcus Aurelius' statue on the Roman Capitol, but even the antique bronze horse near the Church of St. Mark in Venice could have been god-father to them. At least two more works of Italian Renaissance should be named: the great equestrian portraits of Uccello and Andrea Castagno in Florence Cathedral, which one might call painted statues. We return to the middle and the end of the fifteenth century to the states of Donatello and Verocchio. The statue of the Condottiere Erasmo de Narni with the nickname Gattamelata – spotted* cat – was erected in 1453. In 1485 Verocchio was commissioned to cast the equestrian statue of the victorious Venetian General Colleoni, after he had prepared a life-size wax model. He worked on this until his death, and it was only later that the statue was cast after the clay model. How the generations dovetailed is shown by the fact that just at the time that Verocchio was working on the wax model of 'Colleoni', his pupil Leonardo da Vinci

*More properly 'dappled'; from Italian mele = apple. Cf. French *pommelé* and English (d)apple.

36 Donatello. Memorial statue of Gattamelata. About 1450.

37 Andrea del Verocchio. Mounted Statue of Colleoni. 1485/88.

began his designs for the Sforza memorial. Both statues are examples of the pride of the people of the Renaissance, who had taken their fate into their own hands. Rather more restrained but with greater penetration is Donatello's 'Gattemelata' whose will-power appears to come not so much from the physical as from the spiritual. In contrast to this, the deportment of 'Colleoni' is almost a challenge. In style too – quite apart from many details – the difference is plain: in 'Gattemelata' horse and rider are held austerely together almost like a surface relief, while this attribute in 'Colleoni' is pushed vehemently aside; here a joint impulse of movement culminates in the Condottiere-attitude of the rider, whereas in the 'Gattemelata' horse and rider are almost independent of each other, as if the latter found it quite unnecessary to demonstrate that he has his horse in hand.

SO THE THEME of the highly representative rider in Renaissance art emerges – we have seen it already in Simone Martini's portrait of Guidoriccio – and repeated endlessly in the Baroque period, although even then one or two incomparable works of art are found. One is the oppressively magnificent equestrian portrait of Charles V by Titian [38] which shows the Emperor as the victor in the Battle of Mühlberg, which battle extended German lands so far that 'the sun never went down' on Charles' kingdom. There are also the Velasquez equestrian portraits, amongst which is that of Don Carlos [39], showing the Prince on a fiery galloping horse, in which one sees combined with the official business of a court portrait, the unofficial pleasure of a Baroque painter grasping a fleeting moment; moreover it is a delightful piece of painting, no longer involved in the study of details, but enjoying its own freedom.

All these pictures are the surest expression of a new European feudalism in the Baroque period, where almost all the product of art was concentrated at the princely courts. Baroque art is Court art. There is this great difference from the Middle Ages however. These courts did not live by a restricted peasantry, but from the money of the great masters of industry, who called themselves princes, lived in castles and had themselves painted, mounted on horses.
Baroque art also had a democratic side – burgher and peasant. The strength of these was no longer unrecognised but was beginning to come into politics and culture, especially in the Netherlands where a strong merchant class rose against the huge Hapsburg Empire, in whose service were painters like Titian and Velasquez. There emerged also during the Baroque period a democratic art whose great exponent was Rembrandt.
It is characteristic, that this side of Baroque art rejected the horse as a subject. It is rarely seen in Rembrandt's work, never in Franz Hals' or in most of the other Dutch painters. When it does appear, then it is not as an elegant mythological or fashionable subject, but as an animal grazing or ploughing. So – in spite of the mythological theme of Pieter Brueghel's 'Fall of Icarus' [40] the horse turns his back on us: work comes first and not the horse's conformation, the furrows made by the plough are more important than the horse's perfection. Glorification of human peasant work is shown by the lovely soft play of light on the landscape, where the simple scene is taking place. One scarcely notices that to the mythical tendency of this century, the picture renders a small – at any rate pleasantly ironical – tribute. In the mythical flyer Icarus, who tried to go too high and whose wings were burnt by the sun, one recognizes only a bent leg

40 Pieter Brueghel d.Ä. The Fall of Icarus. After 1560.

41 Michelangelo Amerighi da Caravaggio. The Conversion of St. Paul. 1600/01.
42 Peter Paul Rubens. The Prodigal Son. 1618

cal point of view the picture is disunited, the balance is unequally distributed. The huge body of the horse takes up a greater part of the picture. The sacred scene is shown in an extremely profane manner. The 'common people' have broken into the holy circle of art. Dirty hands and feet are more worthy of belief than a well-groomed exterior, and a farm horse is more genuine than a well-bred riding horse.
In an ever-increasing sphere Baroque gives to the life of the people, in all its forms, an artistic value. In Reubens' figures both Baroque tendencies are united: he was a court painter, a much travelled diplomat, and equally a genre painter who never betrayed his vernacular vitality. His picture of the 'Prodigal Son' [42] shows again a Biblical occurrence in a profane manner. In a farm stable there are horses and cows together, simple animals; the horses are heavy cart horses and seen from the rear rather than in 'noble' profile. It is a genre picture, in which this rather ordinary milieu is of more importance than the human ideal, as the Renaissance tried to show and thus a period in which horses enjoyed no social privileges.
INDEED PAINTERS now specialized in specific genre painting, and so played into the hands of the budding art trade, which had to please the special interests of its clients. So there were painters of horses, cows, landscapes, seascapes, interiors and still life. One of these specialists was Philips Wouwerman, who painted the idyllic picture of the dis-mounted boy [43]. Clouds high in the sky, one or two sea birds, a bizarre tree trunk, and horse and rider with their backs to the onlooker, all this lend the picture a soft romantic tone, and it is characteristic of such motifs which recur in the Romantic* period.

*Trans. note – Beginning of the 19th century.

43 Philips Wouwerman. The Grey, About 1660.

LET US PUT Francisco Goya [44] at the end of this chapter, even though this great painter of the eighteenth to nineteenth century did not belong to the Baroque period and only, with great reserve, to the world of the old régime. A new decade begins with him although he stands at the end of an exquisite period of Spanish painting. This painter at the Court of the Kings of Spain was at once and above all, the great – and greatest – painter of that revolutionary force, by which the authority of the eighteenth century was undermined and shattered. He was a painter, not only of the people, but one who took all his ungoverned strength from the people. That he served kings – and after the French invasion even a king appointed by Napoleon – shows the contradictory character of this unusual man. The Revolution took place in France, yet within the formative art of the period Goya was its truest exponent. In France the Revolution took the guise of ancient Rome. France gave herself the attitude of puritanical, pre-Caesar republican pomp and severity and brought into art a new, pathetic, classical naturalism, whose foremost representative was Jacques Louis David. Goya was born in 1746 and David in 1748. Goya did not give up the great artistic culture of the Dixhuitième, 'in the name of the people', as David did, but he carried it over to the new era. There he used it – and eventually exploded it – with an extraordinary passion and expressiveness, with the burning spirit of his personality and with the spirit of the Revolution. Little is gained if one remembers that this painter was of the same generation as Goethe, who was born in 1749, so that his art was an historical 'Parallel' of the 'Sturm und Drang'*

*Trans. note – Sturm und Drang = Storm and Stress, the rebellious, earliest period of Gothe's literary work.

because Goya's art rests on his uniqueness. An encounter with Goya's works in the Prado in Madrid is a breath-taking experience, which the history of art holds ready for us.
From the mass of Goya's works, we have chosen the etching from the cycle of 'Los Proverbios', the last of the etchings which Goya did in the first quarter of the nineteenth century, and in which we are scarcely reminded of Baroque and Rococo art. Amongst the different 'Follies' which the cycle portrays, we show here the 'Folly of Balance'. The exhibition of horse and rider on the rope, gives the idea of a rope dance in an unreal world, which, in this case, is already threatened by the much more real and solid power of the people.*

*Trans. note – The disconnection of a corrupt Court and a people already aware of this power.

44 *Franciso Goya. Disparate Punctual.*
Aquatint from the Cycle 'Los Proverbios'.
1813(?) – 20.

The Nineteenth Century: Mail coaches - Progress - Crisis

HESITATING, unresisting, no longer able to cope with reality, capable only of its social pleasures, dreamily unreal in a world of whose strongest movement they were scarcely conscious, the French nobility went to the guillotine. The shining world of the ancient régime, a culture of indescribable softness, whose substance was more and more spoilt, sank into oblivion. It felled Rococo art with one brutal blow, and with this Baroque art was at the same time exhausted and came to an end.

The horse had earlier receded from the foreground. Until the last moment he had let himself be portrayed with kings, princes and high officers as his riders, but for a long time not with the same intensiveness of feudal portrayal, as at the time of the Baroque. Now no one wanted representative painting; art was to be the pursuit of the enjoyment of life. And for that, parade horses were not required; one needed brilliant festivities and the enchantment of princely salons and gardens; one needed smart charades of every description, and the outward veneer of sensuous banalities. The play of life prevented people from realizing that the reality of life had been frittered away.

And now the place left by the aristocracy was filled by the citizens. They had taken no part in the culture which they put aside, and now they stood there in all their vitality, ready

45 *Ernest Meissonier. The Retreat from Moscow, 1864.*

to secure a new world, but without culture, taste or form. The magic word which humanity put on its banners was 'progress', and with this watchword, with this optimistic certainty, they strode forward from one acquisition to the other, until at last after several centuries, they counted the dismal balance: and of the many spirits which they had called up and of which they could not rid themselves, they had forgotten the essential spirit, and all progress brought them no step further forward.

In this secularity which thought only in terms of horse-power and more horse-power, the horse itself was out of the running. But art, too, had trouble to keep its breath. Money and technique stamped the face of the century. Wherever art gave itself willingly to decorate this undecorative reality, it was inevitable that it would be spoilt. Where she tried to avoid it, there her path remained apart from the great world, on the edge of society which for its part understood less and less what the poets were composing and what the painters were painting. The gulf between public and artist became ever wider. Artists had the wonderful opportunity of great freedom; but they had to buy it with a way of living, which called itself Bohemian and brought as much misfortune as it did charm and brilliance to an emancipated artistic society.

ON ONE SIDE there was an official art, such as our picture of a Napoleonic campaign [45]. The author of this, in the second half of the century, was the then very famous Meissonier, today an almost forgotten painter, who specialized in horses and battle fields and earned plenty of money thereby. The glorification of an aspiring citizenship lies in a monumental figure – the figure of Napoleon. As in olden times a grey

46 Jaques-Louis Agasse. Stage of the Mail Coach to Portsmouth. About 1820.

stallion does his duty. The whole scene has little in common with reality of the past half century, bat more with outward reality in the sense of Naturalism. Painting has succumbed to the power of technique and had so betrayed itself: it had become photographic. At this time cameras were in existence, official painting was at pains to accomplish the same thing with brush and colour and to produce photographic sharp-

47 *Wilhelm von Kobell. Group of Riders on the Isarhöhen near Münich. About 1830.*

ness to the last detail. Such painters, and the patrons and admirers of these monster pieces were naturally deaf to the scornful laughter of those real artists standing to one side. WHERE THE BROAD LIGHT of history did not shine, this did not much matter, especially in the first half of the century, which was not yet revolutionized by technique. As there were as yet no railways, the horse had not lost his function. A certain simplicity, also a hint of unsophistication – opposed

to the heroic grandeur of the powerful rulers – brings us, in spite of Naturalism, to the friendly art of Biedermeier*.
It is the century of mail coaches, for us the epitome of 'the good old times'. So we are glad to see the charming, somewhat stiff-legged but elegant team from the brush of the Geneva painter Agasse [46]. No less are we pleased by the pictures of such an artist as Wilhelm von Kobell [47], who loved painting fine people on horseback, standing still on hill-tops with a wide landscape and free sky behind them – unimportant subjects but composed and painted with care. In such small master paintings there is something of the cultivated art of living of the Dixhuitième, carried over into this century of the middle-class, and especially where the nobility now in middle-class form gives social tone.
THE GREATEST revolutionary amongst the painters of the nineteenth century, and the first, who decided against the tendency to copy everything and to use his own genius, was Eugène Delacroix. Of course, as a painter belonging to the early romantic part of the century, the unusual, the heroic and mythical leanings lay in his blood. But now everything is saturated with personal emotion. No longer is the brush used repressively to study slavishly every detail. The artist has designed with great verve the drawing of the nobleman followed by his conscience [48], where the impression and the emotional pressure are more obvious than detail. This

*Trans. note – so-called from a common but loyal and amusing cartoon figure, 1816-1848 Biedermeier style was influenced by the Empire.

charming sketch lives from the fresh spontaneity of his brush-work, in which a really new artistic freedom is brought out. Perhaps one could object that it is only a sketch. But Delacroix, as scarcely any other painter, relied on the power of the sketch, and he started a period in which people were inclined to value the sketch more as an artistic method, than the finished picture.

ONLY A FEW YEARS older than Delacroix, although forty years before him, is Théodore Géricault, who died as the result of a fall from a horse. He too represented the 'romantic' movement in France. A very keen horseman, Géricault painted horses with knowledge and affection. This 'know-ledge' was brought out in his famous picture of a race at Epsom [49] but it is contrary to his devotion to extreme action. In order to meet similar vehement representations of horses, one must either return to the Baroque period or to the Greek bronze horse of Cape Artemision. The painter tried to unite both exceptional movement and intimate knowledge. For this reason movement is suspended, the gesture of movement and brushwork do not keep up with the tempo. In paying too much attention to detail the fastest movement appears almost as motionless as the slowest one.

HONORÉ DAUMIER was born one hundred years after Dela-croix, and with him we come slowly out of the realm of 'romanticism'. It is false to see only a great caricaturist in Daumier. He was also a great painter, and even his carica-tures show not only delight in scorn and ridicule but often

48 Eugène Delacroix. The Connétable of Bourbon followed by his Conscience. Pencil and brush, sepia, 1835

49 Theodore Géricault. Horse Races at Epsom. 1821.

the knowledge of human tragedy; thus many of his paintings have the mark of tragedy. The painter Daumier was a lonely genius who knew thoroughly the art of every age. With great daring he anticipated much which was proved generations later to be for the general good. One may call him an Expressionist long before the expressionist movement appeared. In an astonishing way he put whole groups together in a simple form; a black and white painter who reminds one of Rembrandt and often of Goya, he made figures simple and with a witty touch increased the effect with the clear vision of the caricaturist for the obvious. Goya and all Spanish painters had at that time a great influence on French painting – this is seen especially in the work of latter day painters like Manet. And so we have here an immortal Spanish subject, Don Quixote [50], which artists selected many times as a theme. Naturally Daumier had to be interested in this mixture of tragedy and comedy – especially in the Don Quixote-Sancho Panza group. In any case, these horses had been quite unknown to art until now. Rosinante, the horse with the sad demeanour, comparable to those horses which are hauled to their feet and condemned to live on after a bull fight, is as 'human' as the proud knight; and beside them is the servant on his lowly ass. So they jog towards new adventures through scenery which one might rightly call 'heroic', if, by the use of this word one did not think of the many 'heroic landscapes' of other – thoroughly unheroic – painters of the Romantic era. But it is decisive, that the horse now is completely in the power of the painter: he draws it, and redraws it; he deforms it to give intense expression to the individuality of his artistic language.

50 Honoré Daumier. Don Quixote and Sancho Pansa. About 1850.

51 Hans von Marées. Lead pencil drawing of a Standing Horse. 1879–81.

HANS VON MARÉES is certainly a painter of another spirit than Daumier, but one could compare his drawings throughout with some of those of the Frenchmen. That this artist is a generation younger than these, and of the same generation as Cezanne, points to different rhythms of development in German art, where in the late nineteenth century, a new classicism is not only accademically honoured, but finds – in Hans von Marées – an artist of the highest rank. In our drawing from a sketchbook of the artist [51] there is certainly little to be seen of classicism. But Marées' art is not concerned with such naturalistic classicism where ideal liberty is in hopeless strife against the demands of exact reproduction. Moreover this artist is struggling inwardly to fulfil the realization of classical ideals, and it is the expression in his art of his struggle which lends his drawings a human worth and an artistic meaning. This is only a sketch of a horse, but it is seen with an inner greatness and designed with feeling. His understanding of the horse's anatomy is clear, but the whole impression lies in the sensitive lines, the many changes of direction, the 'in and out' of the protuberances mean less to the horse's body, than the fact that these lines leave a fine network all over the animal's trunk. So the sketch is obvious and yet there is awareness of the drawing's impulses. The closeness of the fore legs and the width between the two hind legs, is full of artistic tension; and it is expressed also in the short, strong legs and the strongly-made fore-shortened body from which springs the powerful neck and impressive head. With the slight sideways glance, the horse seems to put

an unanswerable question: the question is an element of portrayal. In such a sketch the questionableness of existence appears as an unspoken theme – as it does in Daumier's 'Don Quixote'. But the century is not yet ready for questions; it still believes in facts. The pessimism of a Daumier and that of a Marées are still personal, and do not correspond to general scepticism which appeared towards the end of the century.

ROMANTICISM AND CLASSICISM were soon overcome by the following generation. One did not take refuge in an historical past and a mythical future, but appreciated one's present even if one saw through it. One hated its spirit but one loved its rhythm, its tempo, its elegance and its glittering façade. Since one was not accepted in the salons, then one went around to the studios, the cafés, variety shows, circuses, or the Boulevards, and also to the races. Never in the history of art had horses been painted as they were in Manet's Races at Longchamps [52]. The horses in this picture may be reasonably compared with those of Géricault's horse races. They are full of light and excessive action which the brush has caught – pleasure of movement, pleasure of a fleeting moment, pleasure in colour: it was all optical sensation. People are nothing more than flickering spots of colour, the horses, a whirl of strength, movement and dust. So the generation of impressionists, who were led by Manet, painted. To the actual impressionist the shaking, vibrating movement of light in the air was more important than the noisy action

53 *Edgar Degas. Jumping Horse.*
Bronze, About 1870.

AGAIN a generation, and the century disappeared. The fever of progress vanished, and other realities – economical, social and spiritual – suddenly threatened the world and appeared dangerously in the foreground. Artists could no more optically enjoy the façades, because they had recognised the untruthfulness of sham gold and the reality which was hidden behind it. Neither natural reverence for every unnecessary detail nor impressionistic devotion to the colourful appearance of surface was enough. A new artistic language was needed, which revealed truth behind appearances, which gave form not only to optical impressions but also to spiritual expressions. In contrast to the impressionist disappearance of form in which people had become merely spots of colour, expression now needed emphatic, definite, concentrated forms.

Of course one never met horses behind the façades. They became rarer in composite art. One of the very few who loved horses and who untiringly wooed this subject with brush and chalk, was Toulouse-Lautrec, one of the greatest painters of the 'fin de siècle', and perhaps its most typical representative. He was a Bohemian of noble birth, who 'fell' into this world about 1900, and although he did not 'fall out' with it, he revealed it with critical clarity, without practising criticism, a friend of all those who lived on the shadowy side of life; but he did not allow them the happy brilliance of an impressionist sun: he loved them as they

54 Henri de Toulouse-Lautrec. Jockey, Lithograph, 1899.

were, with all their notorious failings. The lithograph of a horse race [54] shows clearly the return to clear outline, expressively drawn figures in contrast to conventional equestrian portraiture. The horse in full movement, caught in a bold perspective, but not in harmony with 'Leonardo' horses, rather deformed by perspective. One feels that although the problematical is not shown, yet it (the problematic) does touch the horses. These horses, however genuine are no more matter of fact. Life in the year 1900 had shed its self-complacency. It had become questionable, and then suddenly, in the middle of such a crisis the new twentieth century broke upon the world.

JUST BEFORE, in 1890-91, Georges Seurat's 'Circus' [55] appeared. It was the last great work of this master of neo-impressionism, whom one had learnt to recognise more and more as a great painter very shortly after his early death. For a long time he had been taken for a simple pursuer of impressionism, when in reality he counted as one who would surmount it. He was taken for a theorist, who knew more of physics than painting and who took the principle of impressionist colour analysis *ad absurdum*, by systematically subjecting all creativeness to a scientific method. In fact, the rational method which he put in order was only the medium for achieving what was not his perception but his avowal – huge colourful light effects. Because of that he kept himself to the 'clear' colours of the spectrum and to small details of colour, which he did not mix up together, as did the impressionists, but in a well thought out and organized manner, he laid a film of light over the subjects. Simply to speak of Seurat's *pointilliste* method, is to forget that he always took great trouble with form and composition. He was, like Toulouse-Lautrec, not only at the end but at the critical beginning of a new approach to art. His circus picture, with emphasis on form and expression, is a rich colourful composition which eliminates accidental details, such as the impressionists loved, in favour of the strict rules of composition. In the centre of events one sees the white horse, classically inspired, rather too beautiful to be true, but because of that more real in the unreality of the circus tent. On the back of this stylish horse, a doll-like circus rider, hungry for applause, as artificial as the whole glitter of the circus, keeps her balance with grotesque daintiness while behind is the bizarre silhouette of a clown. Another clown appears as an extraordinary trembling fragment in the foreground of the picture and seems to be projecting the scene from between his arms. The ringmaster brandishes his whip, whose crack makes this severely composed painting a surprising 'snap' picture; rather like a film that suddenly cannot unroll further – and remains still as if enchanted. So time stands still, the tired century holds its breath before it vanishes, and a new century with a breathtaking tempo comes in, with which the horse will have more and more difficulty in keeping pace.

55 Georges Seurat. Circus. 1890–91

Twentieth century: the Horse under the wheels of time

IN OUR CENTURY, as we begin to break the sound barrier, the sound of horses is silent. There is not much of the horse left to us. The few farm horses, who still show their usefulness between cars, trains, and tractors, have very little place in our world, nor have the few well-bred horses whose lucky riders enjoy them. There remains for us in the feeling for the beauty, nobility and the kindness of horses only aesthetic delight. The horse has lost even his function of formal display.

Even so, in the art of this century there are still pictures of horses, which are painted not only for aesthetic – or even sporting – reasons to delight us. However, in these pictures today, where the artists occupy themselves with the horse, they do not mean horses: they want to make a declaration – a declaration about our world in which the horse has outplayed his part. This fact alone could be a theme for them: that the horse, in common with other natural features, has almost disappeared under the wheels of time. Perhaps they mourn for something that is gone never to return; but not in the sense of a trivial wish, to want to 'return to better times' which we mean when we think of mail coaches, but in the sense of going back to the natural elementary origin of things. So, for one or other of the artists, the horse may become a symbol, simply for a world in which there are no horses – a symbol of Nature in a denaturalized world. The artists do

56 Wassilij Kandinsky. Lyric. Wood-cut, 1911.

not show horses belonging to farmers or riders: in the portrayal of a horse the fate of Nature is sealed in the world of the people of today.

For this very reason it could never satisfy an artist to show the horse as it is. Because he does not think of the outer appearance but needs to make a declaration, he must use pictorial means to emphasize this. The nearer to Nature a horse is shown, so much less obvious is its symbolic eloquence. It then has sense in itself, it is a horse, nothing else; at best it is an impressive horse, of which type art in the past has given us so many. Present-day artists find no meaning in this. To make the horse speak as a symbol, to make it the bearer of the expression of our manifold world, the artist must change, remake and even distort it. Degas thinks quite unproblematically of the horse's action. With Daumier and Marées a deeper question appears. With Toulouse-Lautrec the horse has lost his matter of factness. From then on it is taken more and more arbitrarily and ingloriously out of its natural contours and proportions, and surrenders to the artist's interpretation.

NOW THE EXPONENT of expression cannot be a horse, tree or flower. Artistic language is now the means of expression. It becomes autonomous until it is an 'abstract' art, which dominates our earth today and where there are no longer horses, trees or flowers. Already at the turn of the century there was – since then – a much quoted sentence, which has kept its illustrative meaning for art of the twentieth century: 'A picture – before being a battle-horse, a nude or a story – is a plain surface, covered with colour in a certain order'. So the whole weight lies on the form, on whose possibilities of expression one may rely. As well for the autonomous language of form as for the spiritual expression, the horse must be changed, even if its outward appearance is sacrificed. Artists have the dangerous freedom to do with horses as they will, but one freedom they have not got: to show them as they are, for by that, neither their form nor their need for expression would be satisfied. As such, the horse has lost its representative power for our world; but the artist still likes to make use of the horse when he wants to make a statement about this world.

We do not want to give here the elements of a history of modern art. We shall simply put a few pictures together without bothering about the position of their historical development. They all come from the first half of our century and they all have an old-fashioned subject: the horse.

KANDINSKY'S PICTURE of a rider in the country [56]. One notes a horse in an extended gallop, with rider, bent trees and luxuriant ground formations: there is action! – but

57 Franz Marc. The Tower of Blue Horses. 1913

not photographic action, rather stenographic action. One of the old masters – even Géricault! – would have paralysed the action with slow brush work, an impressionist would have chased it with flying brush. Here it is reduced to the most elemental tense lines. But actually it is not the action which is decisive, but the splendid beauty of the colourful drawing on the surface of the picture, so that one forgets horse and rider. And this beauty, this enthusiasm for colour and form would still appear, even if the artist ignored the horse's rhythm and remained true to his own inner rhythm for which the description 'abstract art' is an exceedingly abstract name. Already in this still recognizable rider in the country, the artist does not give his picture an objective appellation, but calls it simply: 'Lyric', because the objective content does not count as does the value of expression.

FRANZ MARC'S FAMOUS 'Tower of Blue horses' [57] has vanished since the end of the war – and what a storm it caused when it was first shown! But we need not discuss this, because this art no longer has to be on the defensive. A few horses stand one behind the other in the picture, or rather one above the other. Even in mediaeval times one used up space in this way, but what does it mean? It is the connection of one horse with the other, their common life and fate. 'Animal fate' is another of the artist's masterpieces. And this is similar; fate binds the animals together in curves. They are not free from Nature but joined to her – and yet they have more freedom than we, who, as individuals have fallen apart. The theme is that of the animals caught in Nature's toils; the horses are blue – as the artist wished. Quite decorative, but doubtless there were other reasons for this mode of expression. For a hundred years the Romanticists dreamed of and longed for a 'blue flower', which for them was the

epitome of their highest desire, but it was completely unobtainable, out of all reach even botanically. It is the same with these horses; they are dreamily caught up by Nature, enclosed within the circumference of their existence, into which only man's longing but never man himself, may hope to penetrate. This does not need to stand under the picture as an explanation; one does not even need to 'know' it; but if one submerges oneself in the picture – whether one is aware of it or not – one experiences something similar.

The autonomous language of form, as the exponent of spiritual impressions is clearly to be seen in the picture of Jeanne d'Arc by Georges Rouault [58] with its heavy black lines, like the leads of a Church window, and shining with colour in the darkly glowing glass of a mediaeval Cathedral. And yet there is no sign of an inclination towards the Middle Ages; everything is in the spirit and strength of a modern painter. There is even the traditional type of cavalry horse with raised foreleg; but the horse is seen childishly, simplified, like an earnest rocking-horse. That has nothing to do with the real meaning of the picture, it is all the same as far as the horse is concerned because the truth does not lie in the horse but in the picture – in the artistic veracity. It is truly genuine, too, in the Christian sense, and the work satisfies in that everyone can feel and understand it. Equally indifferent, as a human being is the schematically drawn figure of the girl Joan, like a doll; yet full of expression and holiness. Such holiness is not mimed in deportment or bearing; it lies in colour and form and also in the exaggerated seriousness of the raised head. The expression lies in the pictorial medium and not in the obvious exponents – rider and horse whose forms are overshadowed by the strong composition of colour and form

58 Georges Rouault. Notre Jeanne. 1939.

59 Marc Chagall. The Red Horse. 1939–44.

and by the reserved light, which shows up the immortal light to which this homage belongs.

BLUE AND RED horses are painted by Franz Marc, horses in many shapes and colours by Marc Chagall, amongst them 'The Red Horse' [59]. It is not only because it is red that it is a digression from Nature. It flies wingless through the air, and with five-finger human hands it holds a lighted candle. It has the 'allure' of a circus horse, and over its back a clown vaults as if winging the horse's flight. This is not a secret heavenly apparition, not a vision of the night, and also not – as it well might be – a dream. It is poetry in the medium of painting; it is boundless phantasy; it belongs to all which flies and makes music and is to be found in the air, and in creation and expression of jubilation. And such joy does not just happen; it is locked in the hearts of the couple, who, in tender embrace arise above the roofs of the sleeping town; and it breaks out in wild joy, and the figures who find themselves celebrating this love, fill the canvas.

PICASSO'S DRAWING of a wounded horse [60] is a sketch for the large canvas 'Guernica', which hung in the Spanish Pavilion in the world exhibition in Paris in 1938. Today we have almost forgotten it; Guernica was the first town in the Spanish Civil War which was bombed from the air. Senseless murder, cruelty against blameless animals, all the horror of modern technical invention run riot which has broken over man and animal is seen in the wounded horse, dying horribly. Naturalism is not a language capable of such a cry. The horse's outline must surely burst, the proportions must fall apart, all the harmony of the horse must break down – only the harmony of the drawing outlives the horror. The expression of our time? That phrase comes almost too easily. Marc's

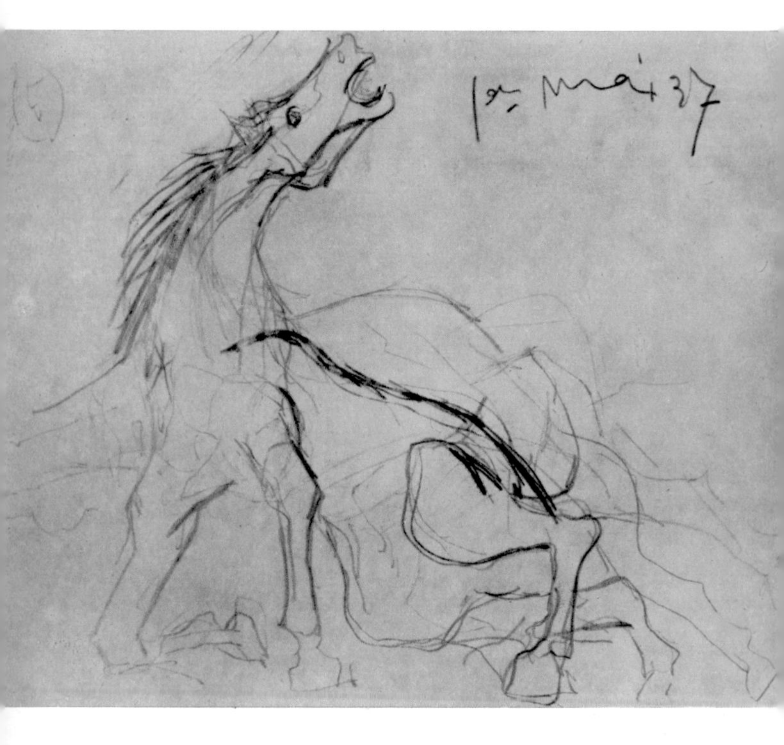

60 Pablo Picasso. Sketch for 'Guernica' 1937.

horses, and Chagall's horses are also expressions of our time – certainly, too, this horse of Picasso.

PSYCHOLOGISTS have recognised that in the souls of the people of today there are 'archaic' stratas, which are overlaid by history and by our own consciousness, but they have remained alive in the unconscious mind, and come out into the light in people's dreams or in hallucinations. In our century artists have undertaken, without consulting psycholo-

61 Georges Braque. Horse's Head. Bronze. 1946.

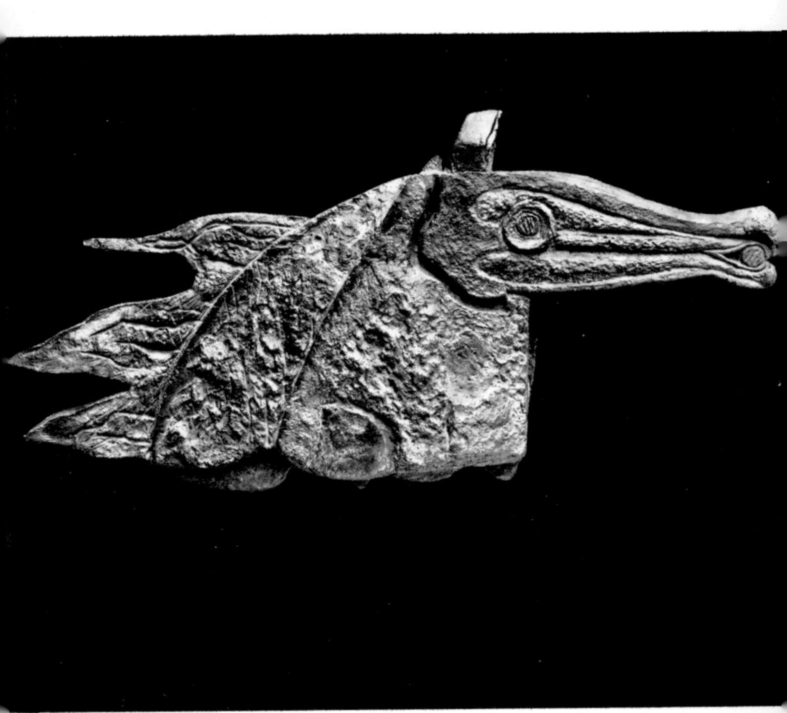

gists and teachers, to expose such archaic strata, and to verify this, one can name many works of contemporary art. This strong inclination to the archaic, which is also expressed in our love of the world's early cultures, is not a sign of escape out of the present, but a submersion into time. The bronze head of a horse by Georges Braque [61] could, by the way in which it is presented, belong to some ancient culture or other. It points to the 'archaic' in ourselves, to that part of the bronze age in us, which has been stilled by many centuries, and 'suppressed' but never overcome. It is a flat relief of a well-bred horse with a small, oddly decorated head and flaming three-pointed mane on a heavy neck, visionary and not quite of this world – 'surreal' and because of that perhaps of mythical origin. But of such significance there is nothing to be said; the significance of this animal comes decidedly from its archaic bearing, it simplification, and its large round eye. Man must have ceased to have much to do with horses, if an artist can create such a horse.

THE SCULPTOR Marino Marini also liked to renew archaic and classical forms, and with one of his works we shall close the ranks of horses [62], not because we see the end of a development or possibly the beginning of a future, but accidentally. We do not hold the opinion that in our day art is returning to tradition or that it must do so. Tradition is not something to which one returns: one lives in it or not; it is not to be relived. Those who have confidence in the works of Kandinsky or Picasso will also feel the reality of tradition, even though it is not in the sense of continuation in the ancient or a repetition of the past. Tradition is no capital from whose interest one may live. In this work of Marino Marini's it may certainly be thought that classic antiquity has been repeated,but that is of no importance to this relief. The only important thing is that which is original in it and he who has an eye for it will recognise that originality is decidedly stronger than the influence of the classic example. These are not antiques, they are Marini's horses, individual, unique even to the modelling of the nostrils, the richness of play of the engraved lines, the plastic rhythm of the chests, the way in which the forelegs are put on to the bodies, in every nervously moulded part of this relief of red clay. Everywhere

62 Marini Marino. Quadriga. 1941.

one feels the complete charm of a 'handwriting' far removed from any classicism.

The outward relationship certainly occurs – relationship with a famous temple relief from Selinuntum or with the Greek pottery picture of a quadriga, which we have shown in our collection of pictures [16]. If we now close our circle – at least the European – then there is no especial acknowledgment to the classics; our love for the Greek world does not require such an acknowledgment at the cost of other values. The acknowledgment belongs to every art, no matter from what culture it comes. There Marini's horses have just as high a place as those of Leonardo da Vinci and many other horses in the history of art which have taken us so gladly through the centuries.

Index of Pictures: